Praise for *I have waited, and you have come*

'Martine McDonagh writes with a cool, clear confidence
about a world brought to its knees. Her protagonist,
a woman living alone but battling on into the future,
is utterly believable, as are her observations of the sodden
landscape she finds herself inhabiting. This book certainly
got under my skin – if you like your books dark and
more than a little disturbing, this is one for you.'
Mick Jackson

'Imaginative, clever and darkly claustrophobic.'
Big Issue

'A story of sexual obsession and broken trust, with
the sodden (and wonderfully rendered) landscape
a constant, literally atmospheric presence.'
Caustic Cover Critic: Best Books of the Year

'It paints an all-too-convincing picture of life in the
rural Midlands in the middle of this century – cold and
stormy, with most modern conveniences long-since
gone, and with small, mainly self-sufficient, communities
struggling to maintain a degree of social order.
It is very atmospheric and certainly leaves
an indelible imprint on the psyche.'
BBC Radio 4 *Open Book*

'An exquisitely crafted début novel set in a
post-apocalyptic landscape. I'm rationing myself
to five pages per day in order to make it last.'
Guardian Unlimited

'Evocative and intrigui~~ng this novel~~
deserves an auc
The Argu

About the author

Martine McDonagh has published short fiction in *The Brighton Book* and *The Brighton Illustrated Moment*. In 2010 she was awarded an Arts Council England Grant for the Arts. She also works as an artist manager in the music industry. *I have waited, and you have come* is her first novel.

MARTINE MCDONAGH

I HAVE WAITED, AND YOU HAVE COME

Myriad Editions

First published by Myriad Editions in 2006
This edition published in 2012 by

Myriad Editions
59 Lansdowne Place
Brighton BN3 1FL

www.MyriadEditions.com

1 3 5 7 9 10 8 6 4 2

Excerpt taken from *Complete Plays, Lenz and Other Writings*
by Georg Büchner, translated with an introduction by John Reddick
(Penguin Classics, 1993). Copyright © John Reddick, 1993.
Map reproduced by Permission of Ordnance Survey on behalf of HMSO.
Crown copyright © 2011. All rights reserved.
Ordnance Survey Licence number 100045474

Copyright © Martine McDonagh 2006, 2012
The moral right of the author has been asserted.

A CIP catalogue record for this book is available
from the British Library.

ISBN: 978-1-908434-12-8

Printed on FSC-accredited paper by
CPI Group (UK) Ltd, Croydon, CR0 4YY

For Gerard and Susan McDonagh

Overhead the heron beats in. The full stretch of his wings rakes the air. His skinny legs dangle over the pond, which is too clogged with algae to offer up anything but a place to go, then drop him to his vigil at the water's edge. He folds his snake-neck into its watchful grey hunch and I move on.

There's a bucket, blown on a gale and snagged by a tree. Pale blue like a patch of old sky that forgot to turn grey, it swings above me, its handle looped over a high branch. I am waiting for the rain-filled weight of it to slide it to the end of the branch and bring it crashing down. Then it's mine; I'm the only one who knows about it and I have it earmarked for a special purpose. But I can't stay now because I've other things to do.

As usual I leave the park by the gate at the derelict lodge, whose crossbars are slippery from the non-stop drizzle, and as usual I hook my umbrella on the top bar and clamber over into the road. The moss-eaten wood bends under my weight and one day will collapse, but for today it holds. The wall on either side of the gate has been demolished and the deer come and go as they please in search of food and shelter, but I'm a stickler; this is how I do things. It's a calm day so I'll take the short cut through the wood, which gets me from here, the park, to there, the market, without being seen. The other days, when it means taking the road, I don't go, because I don't like to be seen. Only one person ever sees me, and it is him I am going to now.

My path, which follows the perimeter of the old golf course, is a fissure visible only to me, and weaves through the shoulder-high ferns like a wonky parting in a thick head of hair.

When we first came here, the golf course was a progression of green velvet swirls. Later it became the makeshift burial ground for the first wave of victims. And when the epidemic and killing had spread so there was no more room underground, or else the earth had baked too hard to dig, I forget which, Jason and his cronies built massive pyres on it, which sent thick foul-smelling clouds drifting over the mill, coating our roof with pestilent ash. I took no interest in those matters then, and I have no inclination to reflect on sinister times now, other than by way of explanation.

So I push forward, and the broad filigree of leaves flicks spray into my eyes. I raise one arm high above my head like a drowning refugee, while my umbrella guides me on through the mud and stones and tree roots that lie in wait to trip me. A raindrop dives from a branch, dodges my hard hat, plops against the back of my neck and sneaks a course between my shoulder blades. My boots, heavy with mud, emit a happy fartsound with each lift of the foot. Any evidence of their fabric and original colour disappeared long ago under coatings of slime. A fern sprig pokes from the buttonhole of my jacket like a marsupial youngster in its mother's pouch.

When I reach the lane that leads to the ruined clubhouse, I ignore it and walk in the opposite direction, towards the road. Up ahead, a pondish pothole spills over the width of the track and into the woods on either side, too large to jump across and – I test it with my umbrella – too deep to wade through. A bent umbrella is no use to anyone, but today is a day for taking a risk so I see no harm in using mine as a pole to swing myself over. As I jump, mucky water spatters my calves. I point the umbrella towards the road to check it for damage, but it remains straight as the road itself, which is admittedly slightly bent. I have become distracted from my mission. Like any human with a purpose, I am prone to diversion. It is one of my worst habits.

I pick up the pace when I meet the road's final sweep into town, but slow right down again at the sight of a reddish dollop in the middle of the road ahead. There's a game I like to play which involves trying to pinpoint the precise distance at which my eyesight deteriorates. In this life, games have to be unwinnable or you have to keep thinking of new ones.

Right now my focus is sharp. The mound ahead is clearly an animal of some kind. A fox or a dog. Probably asleep. I take a step forward. Its outline is still sharp. Another. Sharp. Another. I'm now three steps away, and the shape has blurred at the edges, softened. The change occurred during my last move, but when I take a step backwards again in the slowest possible wobbling motion the precise moment of transition eludes me. It's like trying to watch a flower open.

By its tail I can tell it's a fox. Was a fox. Its head has been flattened, squashed into the pitted road. The umbrella spike prods at its body. Was it you who stole my chicken? Its belly is soft, but more from being sodden than newly dead. I look up and around, but all is quiet, just the creak of the trees and the tiny clicks of twigs hitting the road. I sigh and move on, aiming great heavy swipes at the twig litter with my boots, all the way to the shopping precinct.

No one cared when the storms destroyed the shop fronts, they were already past their best, and in its dereliction the precinct's face is somehow more honest, more suited to the shoddiness of its original, mindless consumerist purpose, as Jason would say. One time, someone made a pathetic attempt at patching it all up, nailed up planks that doubled as information boards to carry notices about the state of things inside each building: DO NOT ENTER! ROOF FALLEN IN! SAFETY HERE! And other more head-twisting messages like: KILL THE PAGAN HAG! But some things just aren't worth saving and they soon gave up.

Before Noah set up the market, itinerants would occasionally occupy one of the safer shops to trade off the accumulations of their travels: home-grown food; hand-made, looted or second-hand clothing; books, candles, tools, herbs and medicines. They would stay long enough for people to get wind of them, exchange what they could, then move on, leaving nothing behind but their stories, which even now circulate the communities in Chinese whispers. Or so Noah tells me.

Now that Noah is the linchpin of the trading community, those same Travellers or their descendants, the temporary dwellers of abandoned vehicles and derelict buildings, bring their scavenged goods to him and exchange them for whatever they need: food, drinking water, clothing. He calls them Jobbers. Without Jobbers, the settled communities in this district would fail. He says.

I duck into my favourite doorway, which I use as a lookout to check the coast is clear before going down to the market. Today of all days it is important I have Noah to myself because what I am about to do is something I once would have considered rash.

An intense, yellow, off-kilter stare from the opposite doorway jolts me back into the present. I step forward, whooshing air through my front teeth, and stretch out a hand to attract the attention of the mange-ridden but still charismatic ginger cat. But he fancies himself as a sphinx too disgusted with humanity to even acknowledge my existence. I straighten up and disguise my intimidation by fumbling in my jacket pocket for the scrap of paper I put there; unfold it to check its eight-number inscription is still legible: *68.36.21.51. Rachel.* I refold it and pin it to my palm with my fingernails.

Reassured now that Noah is alone, I step out into the precinct. Hel-lo. One syllable per footstep, I rehearse my grand entrance. Two steps away from the door I notice the handle has blurred, but there is no time now for games. I take a deep breath, lean my shoulder against the cold metal door and push myself in, to inside where everything is always the same.

Rough wooden crates huddle in the central floor space, some empty and others harbouring the small hard apples or potatoes that are barely distinguishable from one another thanks to their green skins. The combined stink of goat's cheese and damp-brick mustiness hangs in the air and tickles the back of my throat. I clamp a hand over my nose and mouth but too late to stop the volley of sneezes that erupts against my fingers, announcing my arrival before I am ready. Four for a boy.

He sees me first. The only man I know inside a five-mile radius.

'Hello, Rachel,' he says. 'Not seen you for a while.'

Face burning, I wipe my mucous palm against my hip. My over-rehearsed first word sticks in the back of my throat and he beats me to it.

'I hope you've not been sick?' He looms towards me then veers off behind the counter. My head shakes from side to side.

'Have you any cheese?' I say, staring at the pungent wheel of rubbery stuff on the counter. Only bullies and manipulators ask rhetorical questions, Jason would say.

'Only the goat's, but I can let you have four ounces.' He folds his apron into a pleat and wipes his knife in it. 'What else do you need? I think you've still got credit for that last batch of eggs you brought in.'

He looks much younger today than the last time I saw him. But he must be thirty and some men are men by thirty. My courage is on the wane, and perhaps I won't do it today after all; perhaps I should wait to meet someone closer to my own age. And when might that be likely to happen? says the voice in my head. The voice in my head is Stephanie's, but more about her later, because now I am staring at the matted black lengths of Noah's hair, thick and strong, and imagining them, safe as rope, in my hand.

'You just missed a couple of *them*,' he says. 'Unless you saw them?'

Poor Noah, he does his best to interest me in the communities, probably thinks I should live in one. And I do my best to avoid any discussion on the subject, but as usual he interprets my silence as encouragement to launch into his latest story. Noah is never short of stories, gleaned from whoever is passing through, stories about people I have never met and never want to meet. But today of all days I must not give him any cause to picture me in a bad light, so I allow a flicker of interest to show in my face. He pauses for effect before he comes out with it.

'I know what they get up to up there,' he says.

I carry on sifting lentils through my fingers, picking out the tiny stones and throwing them to the ground.

'They make babies.'

My hand stops sifting.

'Momma has them all brainwashed into believing their heavenly mission on earth is to provide beautiful beings for the New Dawn Coming, whatever that might be. And,' he lowers his voice for this bit, 'they keep their men locked up, to conserve their energy for the Impregnation Ceremonies.' He divides those last two words into eight syllables, widening his eyes to add more emphasis, then punctuates them by squeezing one eyelid into an exaggerated wink.

'You'd better watch out,' he says. 'Apparently they're on the lookout for new blood.'

It's a good story, but I take it all with a pinch of salt, not just because it doesn't tally with Jason's grand declarations on the perils of breeding, but also because I've heard these tales before, and no doubt the next will contradict this one. For my own part, I have never seen any men even near the New Dawn house, nor have I seen any children, nor one pregnant woman. But then I avoid the place like the plague. The only evidence of creative activity I've seen is the scented candles and uneven pots they bring to the market.

It's time to turn the conversation round to the real reason for my visit, and with the air so full of talk of procreation my question may seem spontaneous, but I am under no illusion that he will take me seriously; I just have to try.

'I was wondering,' I say.

Wondering. Now the words are out there I want them back. I should wait and find out more about him before I do something so stupid. But Stephanie would keep going, so I do too. 'I was wondering if you would like to meet up.'

It takes him a few moments to realise my mumbling is unrelated to the story he's just told. I plunge my hand deeper into the lentils.

'What, for a singsong or something?' He pauses to cough. 'Do you have a phone number?'

I hold out the damp square of paper, pockmarked with half-moons of fingernail pressure, their shadow embossed on my palm. He takes it and unfolds it without looking.

'Grand, I'll give you a call,' he says. As if it was his idea all along. 'Have you been busy painting?' he says, cutting a rough triangle in the cheese slab.

'Yes. Quite a bit,' I say. Lying.

'Will that do you?'

He slaps the paper-wrapped lump onto the counter and leans his face towards mine. Black lashes brush the top of his firm golden cheek as he throws me a soft wink. I jerk my head back, thinking he is about to kiss me. Embarrassed by my mistake, I stretch my mouth into a too-wide grin.

'I think it might be a bit over the four,' he says with a shrug. 'I never get it bang on.' A second wink implies I hold privileged status when it comes to the measuring out of cheese, which is a start, I suppose. 'Anything else?'

I love the flat *a* of his *annie*-thing.

'Got some nice potatoes in yesterday. Or there's russets still?'

'Oh, no, I've plenty, thanks. I'll have to get going to beat the weather.'

Outside, the drizzle I was too preoccupied to notice on the way in has evolved into a stinging rain that blows in horizontal gusts like swarms of pine needles.

Despite it all the cross-eyed ginger continues to stare into the indeterminate future. I rummage in my bag and pull out a small piece of squashed cheese. 'Here you are, puss.' I want him to like me. I want to be one of those people who have a way with animals. And I want Noah to see me being kind, passing the bit over the four on to a creature more needy than myself. I extend the morsel in his direction and then, when he refuses to take it, toss it at him through the rain. 'Suit yourself,' I whisper, in case Noah's listening. The cheese lands in a puddle close to his front paws. Craning his neck forward, as if the rest of his body has been stuffed and cannot move, he mashes the titbit between rotting teeth, nibbling slow and reluctant, as if his only reason for eating is a fear of seeming impolite.

I push out my bottom lip and blow hard to disperse the streams of rain that slide down my nose. I suspect that Noah misunderstood my proposition. I doubt he'll call. But who cares; at least I have something new to tell Stephanie.

The light is almost gone although it must still be morning. Willing the storm to hold off long enough for me to get home, I pull my hood over my hard hat to shield my ears from the sting of the wind. The rain drums against the umbrella's taut skin and the wind pushes up into its bell, threatening to wrestle it from my two-handed grip. Now it would be too dangerous to take the short cut, I have no choice but to stay on the road and follow it past the House of the New Dawn. Its west-facing windows are bricked up against the weather and all its inhabitants should be safe indoors, so it ought to be easy for me to pass by unseen.

Jason used to work in this house when it was the Vegetarian Society offices, so it was his idea to break in and open it up for the group of refugees whose New York to Paris flight, which turned out to be the last ever plane to land at Ringway in one piece, had been forced into an emergency landing by Hurricane Gilda. Nature's refugees. The sickest passengers from that flight were dumped in the airport hotels, which were already overcrowded but because of their isolation were considered the best place to leave the disease-ridden and dying. So there they were left, with no one to nurse or feed them. Later, when things had calmed down a bit, Jason and his gang set the whole lot on fire.

The healthier passengers divided into two groups. Most chose to continue their journey south on foot, in the hope of finding their way across the Channel, and most of them will have perished en route from starvation or the lack of fresh water. In any case, none of them will have made it beyond the *Wide wide river, As wide as the Channel itself, That once was our great capital.* The rest, Momma among them, were marched up the motorway by Jason, and introduced to this cold and crumbling building and the start of a new life, which they have dedicated to the preparation for something that will probably never happen. And now these memories have triggered my curiosity, which in turn has undermined my sense of urgency to get home. I decide to sneak in for a closer look. If I'm discovered I'll say I'm unwell and sheltering from the weather. Or I'll run away.

This porch was not built to harbour malingerers. The sheets of corrugated iron that cover its rickety frame rattle in the wind and threaten a rusty decapitation. I examine the huge front door; its paintwork is scratched and peeled by hostile weather to reveal the pale oak beneath. Off to one side a wooden plaque announces THE HOUSE OF THE NEW DAWN, in tame rainbow colours. The boards under my feet creak with every move. It's knock or run. Or both. But I'm not yet ready for that level of spontaneity, so I run.

I can imagine nothing worse than living in a community. Nothing and no one could persuade me to leave my island. Not even Noah. In the past, evangelical scaremongers and would-be leaders, I mean Jason and his friends, would pressure isolated individuals to *Join Forces & Share Resources*, and after Jason left I expected his abandoned disciples to target me, but thankfully they left me alone. Sometimes I wonder if anyone besides Noah and Stephanie even knows I exist.

Now the poor old trees are my only guardians and as I make my way home they shake their gnarled fingers over my head like fussy grandparents, reprimanding me for my wayward behaviour. It's Stephanie's fault, I say. We were playing our favourite game of raising the stakes and she made me do it. As if our friendship isn't restricted enough by the distances between us and our connecting satellite, we, or rather she, enjoys putting as much strain on those triangular boundaries as they will take. I just go along with it. 'Come on honey,' she had said in this particular round. 'You *know* what you need.'

It would have been foolish to let on so early in the game that I did know, so I let her spell it out for me. 'A replacement,' she said. 'A lover?' And her voice slithered over that last word, which of course wasn't to be anything like her last word, dragged its last syllable into an upward inflexion. As if I had difficulty in comprehending.

Maybe I did.

'Honey, you're at your sexual peak. Men can smell it, you know. Smell those little menopause-baby butts. But only if you let them within a five-mile radius.'

I giggled like a girl and, clenching the telephone handset to my ear with the aid of a hunched shoulder, shuffled into the bathroom to inspect the fuzzy close-up of myself in the mirror. I have no idea how I look any more; the wall behind me prevents me from putting enough of a distance between the mirror and myself to afford a clear view. I swear I'm going blind. 'But Steph, I have no idea if there even *are* any men within a five-mile radius.'

'My point exactly, honey.'

'I don't know. I've got my painting. I'm happy enough.' I haven't so much as lifted a paintbrush since I used up the last of the paints Jason left but she doesn't need to know that. Add it to the list of things we don't mention.

'Oh, stop right there.'

Stephanie's patience fizzled out even more quickly than usual, and the thought that she might not be falling for it flashed through my mind.

'How many pictures of her own vagina does a girl need?' she said, her voice cracking into a violent cough. Stephanie is sick, but we never discuss it. Her next sentence was delivered on one husky breath, in the brief respite between coughs. 'Now get out there and find yourself a gorgeous young thing with overwhelming Oedipal tendencies and,' she added those fatal words, 'don't dare call me again until you have.'

I was dismissed. For our friendship to be threatened by so trivial a matter excites us both, not least because other, more powerful forces can snatch that choice from us, in a *one false move and the satellite gets it* kind of way.

Nearly home, and the path from the park to the mill is flooding. The fields on either side are already shallow salinas. I jump down from the stile onto both feet and splash black water over my knees and run the full length of the path screeching for joy as each stamping foot shoots rainwater back up towards the sky.

The escalated pitch of the wind has brought the turbine to a standstill. The house is dark but warm. I throw off my soaked jacket and drop it with my boots at the bottom of the stairs, and run up to the kitchen to rub dry my legs with a towel made warm by the stove.

By the time I have found the telephone and dialled Stephanie's number it is too late, the line is out.

The cuffs of my sleeves are wet and scratch at my wrists so I roll them up off my skin while I rinse a potato under the tap, give it a good stabbing with a fork and place it in the stove to bake. Then I dangle a New Dawn spill in the flames and use it to light the New Dawn candles in the living room.

My body is a dead weight, my mind a bag of feathers as I throw myself onto the collapsing sofa, which collapses a teeny bit more every day with the weight of me, then roll myself up in the heaps of blankets and sheets. As the candles burn themselves out, fleeting half-thoughts keep me from sleeping, of Noah, of the squinty red cat, and of the dead fox that I now realise had disappeared on my return. I sleep for two days. I dream of foxes.

Sometimes the wind is merciful enough to anaesthetise you and hold you under in suspended animation while it goes about its business. Other times it forces you to bear witness to its rage, to lie quaking in the darkness, as it menaces the roof over your head, lifting each tile in succession, like a demon tormenting a glockenspiel. Its passing leaves you slumped and drained.

I lie still a while, eyes shut, nose pressed into the back of the sofa, then turn and treat my eyes to the yellow gloom of the overhead light while I fight to untangle myself from the covers that hold me bound. The old oak boards are cold underfoot. In fact the whole room, and probably the entire house, is cold; the stove has gone out.

I hunt for my socks among the twisted mess of blankets, and pull them on. Stiff arms rise up above my head and my body bends forward so that my head is upside down, my nose aiming for the gap between my shins, knuckles scraping the floor, blood pulsing in my ears. I swing from side to side, the knots between my shoulder blades hanging on for dear life, the ligaments behind my knees stretched to their painful limit. In the early days, when my nightmares were at their worst, Jason bullied me into practising yoga, but it seemed the more I relaxed, the worse they became. These days I can never be bothered to clear a large enough floor space, and anyway the premonitions have stopped. Everything that could happen has happened. Or so I believe.

I straighten by grabbing at the table for support while my swimming head steadies, then shuffle across to raise the shutters. Jason insisted on installing the old-fashioned mechanical kind. You wait, he loved to say. You wait, all those fancy remote controlled things won't work when things really get going. He had been no less pessimistic about solar roof tiles: Not much use when the wind takes the roof off, eh? Ha ha. By the end, Jason always talked as if he was getting one over on somebody. It is so much easier to be sentimental about him now he is gone.

I drift from window to window, letting in the grey light. The turbine toils away once more, carving up the gentle southwesterly. Despite there being no obvious signs of damage to the storm wall, I have nonetheless to make a proper inspection. There is always plenty to do after a storm and this time, I promise myself, I will do it.

But I am the queen of procrastination and first I have to pee, then draw cold water into the bathroom sink and splash it over my face. My skin tightens in the cold air. I rinse my mouth with water that tastes of soil, and spit it at the plughole. Bull's-eye. I take the radio from the bedroom and wind it up on my way downstairs, listening to the mechanical drone of the Public Information broadcaster as he reels off the latest storm damage reports: *District Five, floods to 25 metres above sea level, winds at BS6; District Six, floods to 15 metres above sea level, winds at BS6.*

Each forecast sounds the same as the last, but there is comfort in repetition. The weather today will be perfect everywhere: constant drizzle with a force six southwesterly continuing. Or so they say.

I relight the stove, or rather I fill the kitchen with damp wood smoke that sticks to the inside of my windpipe. The sneezes come thick and fast, wrenching my lower back muscles as I twist to prevent the trickle of urine that runs anyway down the inside of my thigh. I blot it with my skirts then stoop to pick a hardened, shrivelled potato out of the oven and throw it in to fuel the burgeoning flames.

Hunger. This hollow sensation in the pit of my belly is such a constant companion that I no longer call it by its proper name or acknowledge its purpose. Unwrapping the cheese, I attempt to drag the memory of my visit to the market across the chasm of the storm and into the present, which is difficult enough. It is even harder to imagine that the events of that day will have any resonance in the future. It is always that way: a storm wipes everything clean and, if it doesn't blow you into kingdom come, pushes you back to square one.

If the radio is working then there's a good chance the phone will be too, but when I dial Stephanie's number the line is still dead. In any case it would be wise to wait until there's something more significant to report, in the unlikely event that Noah should call.

It crosses my mind that if he is keen to see me he might choose to visit rather than wait for the phone. And that if he does, there should be some evidence that I have been painting, of work in progress, or he will think me a liar. Another job to compete for first place on the list that is compiling itself in my head.

I dangle my still-wet jacket by its hood and shake it out into the courtyard, and tie it around my waist by its sleeves. Scuffing my way through tree litter and broken slate to the row of garages that serve as chicken house (occupied), workshop (Jason's, redundant) and log store (seriously depleted), I realise I must have left the chicken house door open because a couple of the little buggers have ventured out and are pecking at titbits blown in by the storm. Their food bucket is empty, but they are happy enough for now.

Hanging from a hook at the back of the workshop is a rabbit skin, ready-scalded by Jason for the making of size. Beneath it is the glue pan with his brown leather gloves draped across its lid, just as he left them. I shake the gloves out in case of spiders then slide my hands in and remove the lid. In one deft movement I yank the brittle, hairless skin from its hook and drop it in. I slam the lid on it, for fear it should magically rehydrate, and make a run for it. I take it up to the kitchen, cover it with water and set it on the hotplate.

I dash from room to room, opening all the windows and shutting all the doors until at last the house is sealed as well as it can be against the forthcoming stench. Finally, I grab a towel from the kitchen and whip it over the banister on my way downstairs so I don't get caught out later.

Back in the workshop I collect the following equipment: one small plastic bowl, one bent spoon, one small lump of charcoal, and a pointing trowel. That the spoon is bent is not essential to the task; it is the outcome of Jason's mind control practice. I use it to measure a few spoonfuls of grey powder into the bowl then tuck the trowel into the jacket tied at my waist. Out in the courtyard I stoop to mix an equal amount of puddle-water into the powder. What I am about to do is tedious in the extreme, but I have put it off so many times that now it must be done.

The wall is ugly, as I predicted, and blocks most of the light from the living room, as Jason promised it would. The outer wall is inaccessible and the gap between the wall and the house is a claustrophobe's nightmare, narrower than the span of my outstretched arms, and boggy underfoot.

Inching my way forward, peering and feeling my way along the wall, I keep half an eye on the ground for hogweed and sycamore shoots. These must be kept under strict control, for reasons that Jason said would be obvious, but which escape me to this day, and as I don't know what I'm looking for I pull up anything that isn't grass or nettles, although sometimes I do pick the nettles to make soup, or tea.

From time to time, to liven things up, and to justify carrying so many tools, I imagine the onset of a crack in the wall's surface, usually at the point where it curves round the northwest corner of the mill, the point at which I feel the first tug of boredom. I circle the spot with a charcoal ring, and then use the tip of the trowel to stir the cement mixture. It's tricky keeping the cement smooth, it begins to stiffen as soon as I stop stirring, but I would rather it be lumpy than keep traipsing back for more water. I spread cement onto the marked area, congratulate myself on the quality of my handiwork and move on.

At the dead end where the wall meets the southeast corner of the mill I collect the ladder and slowly make my way back, checking the wall's upper half. The ladder sinks into the mud as I climb up to mark the furthest extent of my left-hand reach with a charcoal line, as a guide for the next placement of the ladder. See, there is some variation to this task after all. Next time I will begin with the top section because the ladder will be at the starting point.

I flick a little more puddle-water into the thickening cement and stir it in. The south end needs less attention, or at least I am so bored by now that I give it less. Smoothing the sweep of its curve with my hand, I step in for a closer look, but find nothing to fix. Now all that remains to do is to check the tail section that runs alongside the lane and down to the road. To do this I need to cut through the house, where by now the rabbit skin should be simmering down.

I swallow a lungful of fresh air, pinch my nostrils to block out the stink, and run indoors. A door at the top of the stairs connects our landing to the main mill building. I wrench it open and push my way through, gasping for air, into the shell of an unfinished kitchen on the other side, where the cement floor is host to a pot-pourri of broken glass, twigs, feathers and other debris that has blown in through the gaping window frame. A sparrow skeleton, its bone structure intact, lies like an unassimilated fossil in a round steel basin. I pull a ribbon of kelp out of the mish-mash, sniff its salty hide and stuff it into my pocket, then pick my way through the apartment to the solid oak door that is the mill's main entrance. Its bolts work free without effort. I raise the security bar and step out onto the walkway that runs the length of the garage block and doubles as its roof. I stop to take in the view and hold the trowel against my ear like a phone. 'Hello Noah,' I say, 'I wasn't expecting to hear from you.' My eyes follow the tree-lined path that runs into the park, and climb the distant slope to the derelict water mill. 'Oh, yes, I'd love to.' For others words are no more than the tip of the communication iceberg; for me they are all there is. Keep talking, I tell myself, or you will lose the power of speech. Soon after Jason left, an ancient oak, in symbolic gesture, keeled over and crashed through the water mill roof. It grows there still, poking its branches through the broken windows, and from here it looks as if the building was put round it like a jacket. 'Okay then, see you tomorrow,' I say, and slide the trowel into my pocket. Someone is there, in the park, hiding behind the water mill. I catch a glimpse of yellow as they duck out of sight. *Jason?*

In his leaving note Jason said he wondered how long it would take me to notice he had gone. He seemed to think that I had been insensitive to the slow drip of his belongings disappearing, from cupboards, drawers and shelves; but that was me through and through: if I didn't see it coming, then it didn't happen.

He had done everything possible to arouse my interest: sluiced the water filters, fixed the roof, serviced the turbine and held a magnifying glass up to the storm wall. In the workshop were ten wooden panels for me to paint on, the rabbit skin for making size and enough logs and dried food for at least two years.

My every need was anticipated in his preparations to leave, but the day would come when I would be forced to venture off the island. Or die. My choice. What he wanted, he said, was that one day I would wake up to the harsh facts of the present, see things as he saw them, acknowledge and face up to the whole truth of the matter as he saw it. He really wanted me to run after him and beg him to stay. But of course he knew I might not; in those preparations was a relinquishing of control. For him, one future had been realised long ago and a new one was opening up; I was struggling to catch up with the present, he said.

That last day, he lay on the sofa, watching as the ceiling over his head, the underside of the floor that supported me in my bed, melted into the darkness. If only the monstrous chasm that separated our two realities could have been dealt with as effortlessly. It couldn't, he had to leave, painful as it no doubt was for him.

He speculated as to the exact moment I would discover his disappearance. I was in the habit of sleeping through mealtimes so was unlikely to miss him then. But I was always sensitive to the cold; it would be the stove going out and the ensuing fall in temperature that would alert me first. But even then it might take a couple of days for me to fully realise the permanence of his departure.

How wrong could he have been? I knew he was leaving before he did. As Stephanie said, when you live that close to someone you know something is up the second they put their bowl down on the kitchen counter a whisper away from where they would ordinarily place it. You just know.

So by the time he came to write that note, he had already gone; it was his ghost that rose up from the sofa and crept out of the house that last time. How he must have wished that just a tiny part of him, just one teensy cell, could stay behind to watch and report back. But he must have known; he knows me well enough to know I would thrive in his absence.

The movement in the park was probably a deer. I sweep all thoughts of him aside and continue on my way.

The lane is peaceful with the exhausted calm that follows every storm. I pretend to resume my inspection, craning for fissures and irregularities, but my mind is again elsewhere: at the market, watching Noah. I am invisible, a spider clinging to the side of a box of apples. He is talking to someone I cannot see. Telling them about me. Laughing. I erase the scene. Noah wouldn't do that.

Halfway along, the bank is collapsing into the field below; if the lane were to follow suit and disintegrate completely it wouldn't be the end of the world. It is bound to happen at some point. I make a mental note to ask Noah if he knows anyone with a boat they don't want, then splash on through the puddles and potholes, content for once to be having a productive day. I check that the gates at the end of the lane are shut and the bolts running smoothly in their shafts, then relax and enjoy the walk back to the mill.

I take the kelp from my pocket and hang it in the workshop on the hook vacated by the rabbit skin. Drying will draw out some of the salt and impurities. Never eat anything that comes out of the sea, Jason would say. He had a warning for all occasions. Never put anything smaller than your elbow in your ear.

I sniff the air; there is rain on the way. There's always rain on the way. Puffs of steam escape from the kitchen window and evaporate. How innocuous they seem from a distance.

There exists in nature a law which dictates that all unpleasant experiences should become more tolerable with each revisit, but the making of rabbit skin glue never fails to defy expectation. It was always Jason's job, and one that he would approach, for some unfathomable reason, with relish. I see him now, buttoned up in his overalls, waving a wooden spoon high above his already high head, booming Shakespeare at the top of his voice: *The rankest compound of villainous smell that ever offended nostril.* Jason loved Shakespeare. *Titus Andronicus* was his favourite.

Determined not to be outdone, I stride through the mill and suck in enough air to get me as far as the landing. I grab the towel from the banister as I pass, wrap it round my head to cover my nose and mouth and start to breathe again. Quick, shallow breaths at first. Sucking and blowing. The rotten fishy stench is otherwise retch-inducing. Eyes tearing up, my resolve ebbing with each reluctant breath, I lift the lid from the pan and am engulfed in a cloud of toxic steam.

With my towel mask on and the lid held out before me like a shield, I am the rabbit skin warrior. Through the fog comes a bleating sound. I freeze. The telephone. Having got this far I should ignore it, but of course I can't. I start up the stairs and the bleating fades; I about-turn and force my way into the living room and rummage amongst the jumble on the sofa. It's always on the sofa. It is on the sofa. I pull the towel away from my face, press the connect button, and gasp into the handset with my most innocent voice: 'Hello?'

'Hello, sexy.' A man's voice.

'Noah, is that you?'

Silence.

'Noah?'

'Of course. Who else would it be?'

So I was wrong to doubt his interest. He is more flirtatious than ever; I imagine he must be winking like mad at the other end of the line.

'Oh! No one. Sorry.'

'You sound all out of breath. What were you up to, you naughty thing?'

'Nothing,' I say, stifling a giggle. 'I couldn't find the phone.'

My breath should be steadying by now, but it's becoming more laboured, and my eyes are running from the steam.

'You sound excited.'

'Do I? I'm working. Are you at the market?'

I try to pull the conversation back a little, at the same time wishing he would hurry and get to the point.

'No, I'm lying on my bed, thinking of you.'

I wonder if the market is shut because of storm damage or something.

'Are you ringing about our meeting up? I could meet you tomorrow if you like. I mean if that's not too soon?'

I am inspired by my own forthrightness. If that's a word. What else would it be, forthrectitude? He's speaking.

'I have to go over to Edale tomorrow. Can you get out there?'

'Yes, of course.'

I have no idea if I can; it's a long way, too far for me to walk or cycle. I'll have to take the wagon, if I can get it to work. 'Are the roads clear?' I say.

'As far as I know. If they're not I'll make them clear. I'll be in the Nag's Head from six-thirty, then.'

In my excitement, the incongruity of his reference to time is lost. For me, time stopped the day I threw Jason's clock from the bedroom window into the river. When the ticking stopped, and with it the nagging reminder that each heartbeat is a heartbeat less, time became a meaningless, outmoded concept, no more than a word to describe the breaks between storms. I hope the clock in the wagon still works.

'Yes, okay. Subject to weather of course.'

'It'll be fine again tomorrow, that's why I'm going. Got to pick something up.'

'All right then, I'll see you there. I hope I can recognise you away from the market.' Not funny. He doesn't laugh, but he is not put off; he has never heard me make a joke before.

'I'll look forward to it. Bye, gorgeous.'

A click, and he is gone. I wait for the tone then dial immediately. Through the static I hear the phone ringing in Steph's apartment, not frantic like mine but casual, breathing... in... out... in... out... then the ringing stops and Stephanie answers with a grunt.

'Oh, no, did I wake you? Steph, I've done it. I've got a date.'

'You did? Am I dreaming this? Wait while I pull my eyelashes out. Who with?'

I launch into a description of Noah, exaggerating as little as possible, only to realise that the line has already gone dead. I press the connect button again. Nothing. At least the important information has been communicated and our friendship is secure. I toss the phone onto the sofa and return to the kitchen, where the mist has cleared and the contents of the glue pan, congealed into a perfect gelatinous goo, are ready and awaiting inspection.

7.9.43

It has to be Divine Intervention. All those years of searching and hoping and I find it in her friend the ginger cat's den. Eight numbers on a tiny scrap of paper have brought me to her.

4.18am. full orgasm. kneeling.

Today it would be easy to convince me that the clouds have parted and that a white sun is stretching long shadows over the park, awakening dozy bees from deep hibernation, to guide sleepy probosces into ripe stamen. Because tonight I have a date.

I've slept on the bed, by way of celebration, and lie there, my arms waving high over my chest, like a felled tree. The deep blue of the ceiling tints my translucent skin. My arms drop behind my head until my knuckles rap against the wall, then I heave them up and over again to fall either side of my legs with a thud that sends dust plankton swimming up into the light.

I draw the backs of my hands in close to my face, where they are young and unlined. They float away and the criss-cross pattern of my skin, like the imprint of a million tiny birds' feet, comes into focus. Rough and dry from years of neglect, their fingernails scuffed and torn, they are my grandmother's hands. I play the point-of-focus game until my arms ache, then fling the covers away from my body, kick them to the floor and roll off the bed. I rub my hands over my belly, which is hollow even to the touch. My stomach thinks my head's been cut off: another of Jason's favourites, definitely not Shakespeare.

Beyond the storm wall, the river is swollen, the weir hushed and smoothed by the liquid-toffee flood. The sky seems to be made of silver molecules that condense to a soft mist where it meets the earth. I lean out of the bedroom window and rub the fine moisture into my parched skin. I cannot help but wonder, as I do with the passing of every storm, if that is the end of it; if the process of change is now complete and normal service resumed. Normality. Another meaningless concept, a pacifier for the weak and frightened. I trail downstairs, opening each window as I pass. Tonight I have a date.

I throw the last of the dry kindling and logs into the stove to see if they will catch. They will. They do. I lift the lid of the glue pan and press my thumb and forefinger down onto the sticky sky-tinted jelly, spreading them gently to break it apart, and peer down into the rough-sided fissure. Perfect. I drag it onto the hotplate to soften. Its fetid stink is released into the atmosphere in an instant, like a fairytale genie that's been left unsummoned for so many millions of years that it has begun to decompose in the lamp.

Jason's stash of chalk, yellowed and moulded by damp into hard clumps, is in the drawer. I bash it down into powder and mix it a little at a time into the molten glue. The stirring is hard work, and I am soon flushed from the heat and the physical exertion, but as the lumpy mixture transforms into a light cream, so my discomfort becomes the glow of satisfaction. Tonight I have a date. It's like the old days, only I never did any of this in the old days.

The ten panels Jason left, with the outward expectation that I would paint my compromised mural onto them, were really intended to placate his own feelings of guilt. I painted on a few of them, but over time they have all, painted or not, and with the exception of this last one, been broken up for fuel, or traded at the market for something more useful.

I dip the brush into the hot glair and skim it over the coarse surface. A loose hair escapes from the brush, and as I push it towards the edge of the panel a tiny splinter snags my skin. I carry on, lulled into a state of peace by the rhythmic sweep of the brush, and in no time the panel is covered. It will take a couple of days for the gesso to dry, by which time I'll need to have come up with an idea of something to paint, but for now I let the subject drop. A commotion in my belly reminds me my appetite has returned and a trip to the chicken house is in order.

The birds are traumatised by the storm so there is just a weedy trio of eggs in the nesting box, and yet they have the nerve to be hungry themselves. I am convinced there is more going into these chickens than comes out the other end; the last bucket of potatoes I boiled for them was eaten inside of an afternoon. No matter, for now they are happy to ignore me and amuse themselves by pecking around the courtyard for grubs, or whatever it is they find there.

I open up the garage and push out the wagon to charge in the daylight. Jason built it from an assortment of parts gleaned from numerous trips to the vehicle dump, the permanent, rusting traffic jam on the old motorway. It is easy to push, like a big toy. Thick rubber tyres as high as my waist are topped by a long platform with raised sides. Its small yellow cab boasts two seats, the solar panel that generates its power, and three push-button controls: on/off, windscreen wiper, and lights. Its existence is a gross reminder of the horrific purpose for which it was built and of Jason's account of the last day he used it. How the cloth covering his nose and mouth was damp from the sweat that broke in beads on his forehead then ran in streams into his eyes and down his nose, as if every pore of his body were gaping and oozing the very essence out of him. He and his friend communicated in nods; words would not suffice.

Once the wagon was charged with its gruesome load they each took up two corners of a tarpaulin and pulled it over, securing it as best they could for the short journey ahead by throwing ropes back and forth to each other and winding them over and under. The stiff fabric of their waterproof clothing, essential to protect them from infection, chafed their skin and teased out more sweat which dripped and collected in the creases and folds. With that job done they turned to pull with clumsy gloved hands at heads of campion. Then, as they had with each previous load, they stood on either side of the wagon and scattered the petals over the tarpaulin in a gesture of civilisation and ceremony, knowing full well the flowers would blow away as soon as the wagon started to move.

As Jason climbed into the driver's seat and his friend wedged himself in beside him, everything seemed to be melting: the seats under them, the clothes on their bodies, the skin beneath, and the flesh that slid away from the bones being held in check by the tarpaulin.

As they drove away from the town centre, they could smell the toxic black cloud of the pyre before they saw it, above the tree tops, blowing nowhere in the absence of a breeze. The wagon bounced up the drive to the golf course, past the pavilion where the stokers were resting away from the excessive heat of the flames. Unrecognisable in their masks and protective garb, they processed behind the wagon towards the fire for the final unloading.

They removed the tarpaulin and formed a chain to move the bodies. Some were still intact, but most were little more than a collection of dry bones and paper skin with nothing to connect them. Burning was the only option; the ground was baked hard and the effort of digging in the heat with such limited supplies of drinking water would only waste more life.

No one had escaped suffering, and those who remained were imbued with a deep sense of responsibility towards each other and those who had gone. Jason watched his friends at work, well aware that the people whose deaths they were attempting to dignify would have hated to be handled in so intimate a fashion, would have been outraged at being outlived by those they had always considered the scum of the earth, the Travellers and outsiders.

He was exhausted, they all were, their movements slow and heavy. They had worked so hard already to mark out the boundaries of the district to deter the last of the marauders and the diseased, blocking access to the area with barriers built of cars and fallen trees. They had even blown up the dam at Lymm. Nothing could get through. Nothing would ever return to the way it used to be.

Those last jobs, the collection of bodies from wherever they had dropped, the clearing and fumigating of the larger farms and houses for eventual occupation by groups of itinerant survivors, had to be completed before the rains came, because after that the floods would make the work impossible and the spread of disease inevitable. Jason breathed hard against the damp cloth as he dragged the last body off the wagon, its pregnant belly shrivelled and scorched. He threw it on the pyre. Still breathing.

I take my three-egg harvest up to the kitchen to scramble with water and the remainder of the goat's cheese. After eating I lie down on the sofa to mull over the remaining day's tasks and, without meaning to of course, fall asleep.

When I wake again the vague remnant of a dream shadows me, but not close enough to be recalled, or even categorised as good or bad, which in itself is probably a good thing. The light is fading, but I no longer have any sense of the relationship between time and darkness falling. What I do know is that the wagon should be tested before setting out, but I also have to get myself ready, and there isn't time for both.

As I back away from the mirror, and as the seconds decay, so my reflection does too; my hair is lank and flat as ever. Stephanie's favourite words of wisdom nag like an external conscience. Honey, it's all in the hair. Men are like magpies. They like *shiny*.

My hair is shiny all right but not from being clean. What if he wants to touch it? If I wash it, I'll be late for certain. I run downstairs in search of the phone. Bloody Stephanie, why does she have to live in that godforsaken hole? I tap at the numbers, and in two rings have skipped across the raging Atlantic and into Steph's crackling hello.

'Steph, I think my hair needs washing, but I'll be late if I wash it now. What would you do?'

'Honey, you mean you didn't just wash it anyway? You've had a shower though, right?'

I reserve the right to remain silent during this kind of interrogation.

'Oh god. Okay, no one gets anywhere on time these days, he'll expect you to be late. Go girl.'

I've already let her down, not a good start.

'Thanks Steph. Sorry, I'm a bit nervous. I'll call you tomorrow.'

'I'll be waiting.' And it's clear from the tone of her voice that she'll be expecting the worst.

I throw the phone onto the bed. Calm down. He can wait. I try to picture Noah losing his temper, but it would be easier to imagine a day without rain. I breathe in deeply and glide into the bathroom, where I dunk my head into a basin of cold water, then re-emerge with my hair twirled up in the orange cloth I call a towel and stand by the open window and call upon the surging weir to soothe my nerves. But the blast of fresh air teases out the noxious glue-smell that lurks in the very fibres of my clothes.

However badly I smell, Noah is unlikely to notice. He is bound to be carrying the pungent odours of the market on him: goat's cheese and rotting vegetables, their scent clinging to his clothes, his skin, the knotted strands of his hair. I know my own scent exactly, its transitions and phases, overpowering and repellent, warm and sweet, and sometimes I sit with my legs apart just to breathe it in.

The wardrobe door has been closed for so long it has warped and jammed shut. I tug at it with both hands, but it would sooner tip over and crush me than reveal its innermost secrets. With my next effort it comes free, with a nonchalance that suggests it was only waiting to be asked nicely. The mirror behind the door has silvered at the edges and corners. Its general discoloration casts an attractive yellow glow onto my anaemic pallor. Looking good, I tell myself.

My reflection is cut off at the knees. I push the door away for a less amputated, less blurred vision of myself, sticking out a leg to stop it as it swings back towards me. I wobble there, the door resting against my big toe, then let it go and turn to block it with my body while I rummage through the rail of musty clothes.

For godsakes don't wear your pollocks, Stephanie would say, given the opportunity, referring to my painting clothes. Stephanie always wears black, because blondes should always wear black. Does the reverse then apply to me? Should I wear white? In our minds' eyes we have been cryogenically frozen since we last met, whole droughts, hurricanes and tsunamis ago. Our refusal to dwell upon the changes that have been forced upon us is a source of comfort to us both, part of our game. I resort to throwing off the clothes I am wearing and putting them all back on again in a different order. I shake out my damp hair and am ready to go.

Everything I pass on the way out I acknowledge as if for the last time. I am hoping to return with an altered perspective, that after tonight I'll see it all through Noah's eyes, as I once saw it through Jason's. The potential is breathtaking. I wave goodbye to the status quo with a handclap and head outside.

It feels like cheating to use the wagon, but Edale is too far away to walk and to refuse to take it now would be to deny it its purpose. I press the button that starts the engine and it fires up in an instant. The clock is working but I choose not to trouble myself with the convoluted calculation necessary to determine the correct time. The clock in the wagon has always run exactly five hours and twenty minutes behind. New York time. To change it now would seem somehow dismissive of Stephanie, and that would be a mistake given her pivotal role in this situation.

I don't need to know how late I am. Time is an obsolete concept, I remind myself. There is today, yesterday and, sometimes, tomorrow, and if it weren't for the weather they would all be pretty much the same.

A fine mist has rolled over the wall from the river, hangs like a nosy neighbour over the lane and the fields beyond. The wagon bounces and splashes through potholes and over stones, and, although the going is slow, its progress is proportionate to my awakening sense of adventure.

By the time I reach Rushup Edge, the valley below is a broad black pit. In this more exposed place I must battle with the weight of the wind that gusts against the side of the cab. I steer off the main road and up the short, steep run to the crest of Mam Tor. At the top, I switch to neutral and turn off the engine. Below, in the obscurity, Hope Valley stretches an invisible, leering grin.

The wagon rolls forward, slow at first then picking up speed on the steep, twisting descent. My foot hovers begrudgingly over the brake, ready to apply pressure whenever excitement is nagged by common sense. I imagine him below, watching my headlights weave closer. I coast into the dip and lose speed. On the final bend before the village, I restart the engine and creep the last few hundred yards to the Nag's Head. The car park is empty. As I cross to the silent pub, I glance a wish up to invisible stars.

I lift the latch and stand in the open doorway. Once upon a time, this pub was the focal point for a whole community, albeit a diverse and transient one, its long tables crammed with chattering families and groups of walkers thawing out at the end of a long day's hike, passing around chips for communal dipping. Hot toddies and mulled wine soothed their bones and warmed their aching muscles. A long time since.

One brave step forward reveals that a log fire is still blazing away in the snug. Two men on high stools sit at opposite ends of the bar. One of them directs a murmured comment towards the other via the barman who, leaning with his elbows on the bar reading a news-sheet, catches each word and passes it on verbatim, as if the language is no longer strong enough to manage the full distance unaided. No one looks up. With no talking or action to move it around, the air is as still as in a painting. A Hopper revisited in yellow and brown. I am the character you cannot see, just out of frame.

At last, the barman raises his head to look in my direction, which is sufficient encouragement for me to give up the safe haven of the doorway.

'What can I get you, love?'

He doesn't seem to find my arrival at all odd. Perhaps he has been told to expect me.

'I've only got brew.'

Noah sometimes has brew at the market but I've never tried it. As there's no alternative I order a small glass. It didn't occur to me to bring anything with me to trade, but he seems not to mind.

'I'll bring it over, love. Where are you sitting?'

I point towards the snug, then turn to follow my own directions, choosing a seat at the table closest to the fire, not so much for its warmth but because I imagine it will look good to be engrossed in watching the flames when Noah arrives.

It is only when I turn to thank the barman for bringing my drink that I realise I am not alone.

36

'Excuse me,' I say to the barman, 'is there anyone in any of the other rooms?'

'No, love, they're all shut up. Waiting for someone, eh?'

I smile my reply and the barman moves away.

Backed into the far corner of the snug is a man, the top of his yellow head illuminated by a flickering wall-light. His skin is insipid and green-tinged, and, while his eyes are wide and angry, the generality of his face is of little interest to a painter such as myself. A downcast shadow hovers over lips devoid of blood or passion. I turn away casually as his eyes flick in my direction.

'Excuse me. Are you Rachel?'

His voice is not unpleasant and has a power and depth out of keeping with his appearance. I look back at him but say nothing.

'I'm a friend of Noah's,' he says. 'He's going to be late. He asked me to come and let you know. Keep you company until he arrives.'

I continue to stare. The man stands. He has my attention.

'Do you mind if I join you?' He moves towards the fire. 'I'm sure he'll not be long.'

The reflected glow of the flames lends a false vitality to his cheeks. He waits a few moments out of politeness, expecting my invitation. When none is forthcoming, he moves in behind me anyway. The screech of a chair being scraped over the flags stings my ears. One of the men at the bar throws a disinterested glance in our direction.

Seated now, Noah's friend extends a hand across the table, which I pretend not to see.

'White. Jez White.' He smiles. At full stretch, his mouth measures no more than an inch and a half across. I muster a hello in return. His glass is empty. I return to my flame-watching, ignoring the pressure to engage in conversation, until his presence annoys me to such a degree that I am forced to speak.

'There's no need for you to wait, I'll be fine, thanks.'

'It's no bother.'

Another smile, which I don't acknowledge because I am busy pondering how different it would be if Steph were here, or Jason. They would know how to get rid of him. But of course if Jason were here then I wouldn't be, or at least not for the same reason. So he stays put. Keeping his stare constant in my direction, he cuts a criss-cross pattern into the edge of the table with the nail of his index finger.

'How do you know Noah, then?' I say, keeping my gaze on the fire.

'We worked together at the solar plant in Warrington, before the floods, like, and when he was on the road. He's said some very nice things about you.'

I conceal my surprise. 'What do you do now?'

'I'm a sculptor. I survive,' he says. 'Do you do anything?'

'I'm an artist too. A painter.'

'What do you paint, then?'

'Landscapes mostly these days.'

I wish I'd kept quiet.

'What about people? How would you paint me, for instance?'

I deny myself the pleasure of telling him it would be hard to find a less fascinating subject; he is after all a friend of Noah's, and it might get back.

'Well, as all I know about you is your name, I would paint you in white, in a white room, like a ghost.'

'Mmm, I like that idea. You must be a great artist.'

His tone is devoid of flattery, accompanied as it is by a smirk that hollows his cheekbones. I lift my glass to my lips; the body of my drink turns crimson in the firelight. He's not finished. 'So then, are you in the camp that thinks the Impressionists were just a bunch of short-sighted realists?'

I consider leaving, but then the pub door opens, as if nudged in by the breeze, and I turn an expectant blush towards the newcomer. But it is an elderly man who enters the bar, neck bent so far forward that his eyes see nothing but the stone flags passing under his feet. He raises his stick an inch off the ground and waggles it in greeting, first in the direction of the bar, then towards the snug. I smile to myself and turn back to the fire. A slow roll of voices starts up behind me and eases the tension.

'Would you like me to check if there's a bedroom available for you? Perhaps you would rather wait upstairs.'

'No, it's fine, thanks.' I down a large swig of brew. If he won't go then I will. 'I think I'll go home now. I'm not very good at waiting.' I stand, a little wobbly from the brew. 'If Noah turns up, please ask him to call me.' Then, remembering my manners, 'It was nice to meet you.'

'Night love,' the barman calls as I raise the latch on the door. I turn to wave but if he even looked up to speak he has already lowered his head back to his news-sheet. The old man raises his stick in farewell, but not his eyes.

The night is darker than ever after the pub's glow. Clouds have thickened overhead, herded together by the roiling wind. I hurry to the wagon, resisting the urge to look over my shoulder. I open the door and climb in, slam the door and start the engine.

The turbines beyond Rushup loom like ghosts out of the darkness, their blades motionless in the squally wind. It would have been safer to stay at the pub. If the wagon runs out of power now I will be in serious trouble. By coasting down the hills I should be able to conserve enough power to get me home. I hold my breath to suppress any show of disappointment, even to myself, but a pricking sensation fizzes at the tips of my fingers. By the time I reach the gates at the end of my lane, the wind is howling enough for the both of us.

8.9.43

*She threw back her head, my beautiful Paloma, so that
her body moved in one swooping swerve from bending to
upright. Her glossy black hair fanned out like a peacock's
tail then tumbled, poker-straight and glistening, onto her
perfect shoulders. She will come to me slowly, in her little
yellow wagon. I will place my hands on top of her head and
let them slide, all the way down. My beautiful dove, my
sparkling Paloma, she stood in the doorway, expectant as
a new arrival at a party, waiting to be announced. But no
one rushed forward to greet her, not even me. Poor Paloma,
she had to make that first step towards the realisation of
our shared destiny alone. Is it more than I can hope for
to feature in her thoughts for just a fraction of the time
she occupies mine? There is an attraction between us that
could fire a whole community for a year, so powerful we
can hardly bear to look at each other. No words can express
our primal bond; it has existed since the birth of time. We
are Adam and Eve. And Noah is the snake. I will banish
him from her thoughts. She is beautiful and shy, just as I
predicted she would be, but clear and confident too. I need
to see her once more and then she'll be mine.*

3.18am. ³/₄ orgasm. kneeling.

5.22pm. full orgasm. standing.

Outside, the poltergeist wind hurls itself about. With each gust raindrops clatter against the shutters, as if a million marksmen, lined up on the canal path beyond, have cocked their bows and released their arrows at my window.

Under siege. I stand in the centre of the living room, staring at nothing. The dim yellow bulb flickers overhead, its feeble impact on the gloom serving only to accentuate the room's dark corners. I swivel round to fix my gaze on the panel that leans, like the insolent stranger it is, against the wall. The size lends its surface an unnatural softness, has transformed the rough to bumpy smooth. I dab at it with a finger. Jason would have insisted on applying another coat, but I don't have the energy. Instead I collapse onto the sofa. Today's determination has become tonight's diminished resolve. I pick up a book, my only book, from the floor. It's too dark to read, but just holding it brings some comfort, the light pressure of it against my chest reminds me that at least I'm still breathing. My eyelids droop. I roll onto my back and lie still. The book dangles unopened at the end of my outstretched arm, then falls to the floor.

A clap of thunder fit to herald the end of the world wakes me. My eyes open wide, blind in the pitch dark, my heart thumping in my ears, breath locked into my lungs. I dare it to come. I dare it to come and get me. It comes. A rumble rolls in low from the distant west and cracks the sky directly overhead, wrenches it apart, shakes the island to its root. And then it bursts; a symbiotic concoction of wind and rain explodes against the shutters. My eyelids droop again in relief. But I shiver in the temperature drop. I've been static for too long.

Underpinning the elemental discord is my own breath, each beat in its regular easy rhythm a pathetic stab at stability. I force myself back into a slow doze, into a dream of being watched. The watcher, like a lonely sun, devours my every move, exposed in a bleached landscape where escape and shade are wistful memories. The shutters rattle me awake again. This storm does not allow sleep.

My feet twist to the floor, and with eyes squeezed shut I feel my way across the room. Every day my sight deteriorates a little more. One day I'll go blind from living so long in the half-light. Would my life really be so different? The unknown is the unknown whether you can see or not.

My hands locate the torch, fumble for its handle and begin to wind, my weary muscles grateful for the brief rest that follows each click as it turns. I flick the switch and it casts its wide yellow eye onto the sofa. I climb back under the covers to read, with the torch wedged into the gap between wall and sofa, illuminating the well beneath my chin.

I push the book up into the beam and inspect the fluffed paper at the corner tips, and the cracks and flaws that emboss its otherwise smooth surface. I part the pages at random, an action so habitual that the book always falls open at the same place. Chance has become certainty.

Without flicking forwards or backwards from this random point, I read aloud to myself. My eyes rest briefly on each word, more from a sense of obligation than the need to communicate them to my mouth, then pass on. This tale is so familiar; at least I will still be able to read to myself when I do eventually go blind.

> *Once upon a time there was a poor child, had no father and no mother, everyone was dead and there was no one left in all the world. Everyone dead, and the child went out and cried both day and night. And, seeing there was nobody left on earth, she wanted to go up to heaven, and the moon gave her such a friendly look, and when in the end she came to the moon, it was a lump of rotten wood, so she went to the sun, and when she came to the sun, it was a withered sunflower, and when she came to the stars, they were tiny golden insects, stuck there as though by a butcher-bird on blackthorn, and when she wanted to come back to earth again, the earth was an upturned cookpot, and she was all alone, so she sat down and cried, and she's sitting there still, all on her own.*

I read to the end of the passage three times, comforted by the sound of my own voice. I have never experienced loneliness, never felt it as a tangible presence. I close the book, switch off the torch, place them both on the floor and wait for sleep. For sometimes sleep is the only way of passing from one end of the day to the next.

I dream on oblivious, even as the wind subsides to a harmless whisper and the overhead light flutters back to life. When I do wake, I mistake the pounding in my head for the continuing storm.

I squeeze my eyes into a tight clench and let them spring open again, but the pain has already taken root. I roll off the sofa onto all fours, pull myself up and shuffle towards the warmth of the kitchen, where there is nothing to eat. I flop downstairs, pull on my boots and hurry across the courtyard. The yellow-grey storm light lingers. Or it may be the approach of night.

There are three eggs again. I take them in and set them on the stove to cook; the pan lid rattles in the sporadic puffs of steam that erupt from the eggy mess below. Meanwhile I go upstairs to raise the bedroom shutters.

As the heavy blinds creak up into their rests, a movement on the canal towpath catches the corner of my eye. I turn my head in its direction, expecting to witness the languorous swoop of the heron, but instead my curiosity is rewarded with a rare sighting. Up on the path is a man, his coat, luminous against the grey sky, flapping in the breeze. Raindrops race across the windowpane like sperm towards an unfertilised egg; a living, moving curtain that separates me from the outside world and distorts and bends the stranger out of shape. I daren't open the window for fear of being seen, but peer across. At this distance I cannot tell which way he is looking. Nor is there evidence in any direction of anything likely to attract and hold his attention so. He has no umbrella. Maybe he is lost. I could call out, offer him shelter, but don't.

A distant rattling demands my attention. The eggs! I take the stairs two at a time, then, stifling the heat of the handle with a towel, scrape the pan from the hotplate. I make for the stairs again, shovelling a spoonful of egg into my mouth as I go. The metallic aftertaste of the spoon makes a stronger impression on my tastebuds than the food does. My foot catches against the riser of the top stair and I lurch forward onto the landing. The spoon hits the floor. By the time I have resumed my position at the window, the stranger has gone.

I open the window and lean out for a longer view, but whoever it is has vanished. Whoever it is, he is not getting away. I scrape into the blackened crust at the bottom of the pan and force the last of the egg down my throat, then dump the pan on the floor and rush to find my jacket and go out to the park.

Once a luscious paradise, the mansion gardens are now an impenetrable jungle, raped and pillaged of their once-famous diversity by the rhododendrons that have smothered everything in their path. The meconopsis bed no longer winks a fragile turquoise gaze at the sky, but is reduced to a miniature forest of short hairy stumps that taper from green to sodden black. The lawns are a spawning ground for the elephant plants and flag irises that creep inland from the lake and at certain times of year, no longer determined by the seasons, are a moving carpet of baby frogs.

A few anaemic petals cling to the wiry twig of a rose bush. The notion that the stranger may be watching nearby affects my behaviour. I reach up and pull the inadequate bloom to my face, attempting to light my eyes with the inspiration of one destined to paint all the colours missing from the world. In my fervour I dislodge the petals and watch them float earthwards while the remaining woody bobble comes away in my hand and the thorny spindle, relieved of its burden, springs back to dance and nod in the swoop of the breeze. I look casually about, rolling the rosehip in my palm, and then toss it towards the nearest puddle. It lands with a click on a floating leaf. I look around again. No one.

In the vegetable beds the feathery tops of the carrots are already filling out. I twist one with both hands until it breaks, and push it into my mouth. Saliva spreads its bitter juice over my tongue; tiny green hairs embed themselves in the cracks between my teeth. I dismiss my imagined audience by spitting a large globule of bright green mulch to the ground.

I take measure of the encroaching dusk and decide there is time enough to dig up some potatoes before nightfall. I remove my jacket and spread it on the ground, then lift the fork, stab it into the earth, and press all my weight down onto the handle. Working it backwards and forwards I push it deeper still. I try not to think about Noah, but everyday tasks are so much more enjoyable when there are more confusing matters to be distracted from. I pull the handle low to the earth, and watch the plant at the other end rise up. Then, anchoring the fork with my foot, I grasp the plant by its stem and shake it off. A mix of earthy clods and young potatoes drop back into the ridge. I throw the leafy part over my shoulder and root around for the spuds, free them from the clumps of soil that encase them and toss them onto my jacket.

When I'm done, I tie the hood and bottom of my jacket together to create a makeshift sack. I tie the sleeves round my middle to hold it securely in place and clutch the bundle to my belly like an instant pregnancy. The yellow eye of the torch guides me out of the gardens. If anyone is near they will surely see me now. But no one comes. I am alone, and my solitude stretches around me and into the distance as far as the eye can see.

The phone is ringing as I stumble through the mill; it is still ringing when I run up the stairs. Let it be Noah. I throw myself onto the sofa, potato bulge and all, and summon up my sweetest voice.

'Hello?'

'Where've you been? I've been waiting for you to call me.' It's Stephanie. Stephanie never calls me.

'Oh god, sorry, Steph. I did try but the lines have been out for days, what with the storms.'

'So, what happened?'

'Um... just a minute.'

I put the phone down to loosen the sleeves round my waist and let the potato bundle drop to the floor. Spuds roll in all directions. 'Sorry, I've only just got in.'

'Is *he* there with you?'

For Stephanie the use of a telephone is a mere formality. Her whisper is louder than a normal person's shout.

'I mean, how'd it go?'

'No, of course he's not here. It went fine.'

'What d'you mean it went fine? Did you sleep with him?'

'Well, no, but we both wanted to.'

'So what was stopping you? Public opinion? You liked him, right?' There is no time for me to answer. Stephanie quick-fires another question right over the top of the last. 'And he likes you?'

'Well, I assume so. He asked to see me again.'

'Great. You even kiss him?'

'Yes.'

Oh god, here we go.

'On the lips? Where?'

'Steph, this is like the Spanish Inquisition.'

'Sorry hon, but outside of the obvious, this is the single most exciting thing that's happened to me for years. I need detail.'

I pause for a second to wonder why it is that whenever I need time with Stephanie the line always cuts out, but today, when I am slow-witted and dull, when I have dug myself into a hole I can't easily clamber out of, I have all the time in the world. There's only one thing for it. I press the connect button and cut her off.

I bury the phone under the blankets on the sofa, so that if it rings again I won't hear it. I never thought I could do such a thing, not to Stephanie at any rate. I don't know why I even bothered with Noah in the first place. I should have just made it all up from the start. That way I could have kept control of the situation and entertained Stephanie at the same time. All I can do now is hope to hear from Noah soon so that my lies can be made prophecy.

The day is bland and warm as summer, a fine drizzle issues from a plain white sky, and in fact, if you were just going off the look of things, it could *be* summer.

The phone is ringing. I drop the bucket and it hits the ground with a clang that sends the chickens flapping and squawking away. It's probably Stephanie, in which case I am ready with the final thread, which will tie the bow on my little pack of lies. Why not? It will only make her happy to think of me in love; will make her think she is winning. All the same, a worm of discomfort in my stomach makes me hope it isn't her. I don't like to cheat. The chickens jostle in on the spilled potatoes, pecking at each other in their desperation, the weak butting the weaker with their puny chests. I get to the phone, out of breath.

'Hello, Rachel, it's me, Noah.'

'Oh.'

'I'm ringing to apologise about the other night. The chain broke on my bike. I hope my friend looked after you. He thought you were lovely.'

I resist the temptation to tell him his friend's feelings are not reciprocated. Nor can I quite summon the energy to be cross with him.

'Can we make another date? I'd love to make it up to you, if you'll let me?' He hesitates, waiting for a response that doesn't come. I want him to suffer as I had to in the company of his hideous friend. 'How about tonight... Are you there?'

'Yes, okay.'

'Good. At eight?'

'All right,' I say. 'Where?'

'I could come to you?'

'No. I don't think so.'

'Then how about Alderley Edge; we could go for a walk or something?'

Or something. Most of my waking hours are spent wandering about; it isn't really what I would choose to do for romantic entertainment, but put on the spot I am unable to come up with a better suggestion. Maybe that's what people do now, couples. What else is there?

'Okay then,' I say. 'I'll see you there.'

The chickens have made short work of the potatoes and are now scattered about the courtyard, pecking idly at the ground or engaged in the preening of ragged feathers.

I scrape up mashed lumps from the ground, each one embossed with the skeletal imprint of a four-toed culprit, and scoop them into the bucket.

Given the excited, hope-filled hours that preceded my rendezvous at Edale, and the disappointment that followed, the most I can allow myself now is an uplifted sense of resignation. I wipe my sticky hands on my jumper. Alderley Edge. Closer than Edale but still miles away.

The panel is ready for painting, but the thought of starting work induces an overwhelming lethargy. My mind sifts again through previously discarded ideas and rejects all of them for a second and third time. There's no reason to paint any more. There are no more stories to tell, and no one to appreciate them if there were. No matter which direction my thoughts follow, they are consistent only in the pattern of their wanderings and their ultimate destination: pick up a wave, ride it, then tumble full circle to land slap-bang in the middle of self-pity. It must be the weather. I return to the house for a nap.

The ringing phone wakes me. It's probably Noah with some flimsy excuse. If I don't answer he won't be able to blow me out; he can't let me down twice. So I don't answer. I shift my attention to the stagnant air that hangs warm and moist at the open windows and wait for the ringing to stop. My body is sticky on the outside but my insides are chilled by sleep. I roll onto my back and stare at nothing, scanning my insides for some indication of how I might be feeling. When nothing occurs to me I roll reluctantly to the floor, crawl to the window and pull myself to my feet.

I close each window in turn, winding the shutters down as I go. Then, unable to find any further excuse to delay my departure, I leave the house.

As I pull in at Alderley Edge, I notice the outline of another vehicle, hidden in the shadows on the far side of the car park. Square and sleek with blacked-out windows, this type of car was banned long before the burnouts. I park close to the exit, as far as possible from the other car, in case someone is living in it and my arrival gives them a fright.

I switch off the engine and the world falls for a moment into silence. A silence that is immediately broken by the crack of the other car starting up, which cuts through the peace like a mistimed echo. The car inches backwards, and creeping night reclaims the void beyond the flare of its headlights. In my rear-view mirror, I watch its languid shadow spread deep into the woodland.

The car ignores the exit and instead swings round, sending a sweep of reflected light across my face, and crunches to a dead stop alongside the wagon. I stare straight ahead, my ears picking up the thud of the car door and the scuff of the driver's feet on the uneven ground. My fingers rest lightly on the door handle at my side.

A human shape fills my side mirror. I push open the door and step out, raise my eyes in readiness to greet Noah's soft brown ones.

'We meet again.' Jez White grins.

My hand refuses to let go of the closing wagon door. I glance over his left shoulder, hoping to see Noah emerge from the passenger side of the car. But both doors remain shut and its blackened windows offer nothing but my own gaunt reflection. All colour negated by the night.

'Lovely night,' he says, lifting his chin towards the sky while keeping his eyes fixed on my face. He is almost my height. His dirty blond hair is weaker and thinner in the moonlight; a smile twists his mouth out of shape. I hold his stare to mask my irritation.

'Where's Noah this time?' My words allow my eyes to stray from his without admission of defeat.

'He shouldn't be long. I told him I would wait with you until he gets here. It could be dangerous out here at night.'

Then why would I feel safer alone? I shift my weight into my right hip. He stands fast. Questions squat in my mind, ready to pounce should my mouth open, but no such opportunity presents itself. In the tally of status points White is winning, and he cannot resist exploiting his lead.

'He said if we're cold we should start walking and he'll catch us up. I've brought a flashlight.'

My glare is enough to slow him down, but not to discourage him.

'Or we can wait here, of course.' He gestures towards his car.

I find a word. 'No.' And then another. 'Thanks.' My eyes remain fixed now, not leaving his face for even a moment, penetrating, gaining ground. I refuse to be intimidated by this little man. But when will it be all right to stop being polite to him? At last he looks away and I jerk my hand down on the door handle. In a whisper the door is open and I position myself at the wheel. White turns back, amused, and leans forward to peer in at me. Laughing. His face is so close it's a blur. I force a smile and raise a hand to the window. His hand reaches for the door, but he is too late. The wagon jerks backwards, compelling him to step away.

If Noah is really on his way then I'll pass him coming up. I try to focus my attention on the road ahead, but my eyes persist in flicking to the rear-view mirror. No sign of White in pursuit. Nor is there the tiniest speck of a bicycle lamp ahead. The wagon's battery is losing its charge and the headlights are fading as the wagon drifts homeward past looming houses that are restored momentarily in the bluish light of the headlamps, which reglaze windows, retile roofs and renovate whole buildings. The mangled cars that stand in their driveways, the redundant machinery of past lives, are testament to the reality of an inescapable past. Driving slow. Or anti-fast. The obsessive belief in the value and power of speed, which once confused the blurring of things one would rather not see with progress, has at last been recognised as folly, at least by most.

At last the appearance of the park wall at Dunham rouses me from my thoughts. I jump out of the cab to haul apart the gates that are the final barrier between safety and me, and drive through without stopping. I park in the lane, clamber up the steps to the walkway. Home. Where, through sheer force of will, I submerge myself into a worrisome dream, in which a thin, fragile version of myself, lit by an intermittent moon, creeps barefoot towards the gates. The wind howls, but I am deaf to its warning and continue with my creeping, head down, hair streaming. I call to my dreamself to turn and go back, but she doesn't so much as look up. I am swallowed up by the blackness until I am no more than a pale glimmer of life, creeping, creeping. Trees crash around me, blocking my way, but nothing can deter me. The river hurls itself at the wall, but I am at the gates now, and the wind is too strong and the gates too heavy. I cannot pull them all the way to. All my strength cannot shut out the storm. I turn towards home. A car's headlights appear in the gap between the gates behind me, stretching my long thin shadow back to the mill, weakening me. The trees and the wind and the water are quiet. I stand alone in the light.

Sweating, heart racing, I scramble to my feet. I left the gates open!

The mill is deserted and silent but for the wavering beam of my torch and the chirrup of baby mice. Out on the walkway the weather is unchanged; the only sound is the surging applause of the weir. The charm of my surroundings is not lost in the moonless night and I breathe it in for courage as I stride out into the lane and canter towards the gates. Imagining the purr of a car engine somewhere beyond the park wall, I accelerate to a sprint. I haul each gate in turn, sweeping two ridges of earth and stones into the lane. One final wrench and the gates meet. I ease the bolts home and rest my clammy forehead against the cool metal. This is all Jason's fault.

9.9.43

Even in the night she shines.

1.08am. $^3/_4$ orgasm. missionary.

Another two days and nights pass before the weather is calm enough for me to make the journey to the market. I fidget my way through, mixing paints, making bread, and planning Noah's chastisement. Ideas circle my head like midges, shadow my every move but never land. Words change direction with the wind. The fantasy is this: Noah's contrition, provoked by my feigned reluctance to accept an apology, allows me to gain advantage over him.

But when at last I barge into the market, without even stopping first to check if he is alone, the reality is so different from the fantasy that I could never have been prepared for it. He smiles and waves as usual, even winks, without a hint of self-reproach, his 'Hello Rachel' is as sweet and calm as you like.

I respond in a dry monotone, to let him know he is out of grace, and it works; he stops smiling immediately and launches his defence.

'I'm sorry I haven't called. Only I've been busy. And when I have had time, the phones have been out.' There is an edge of panic in his voice, which I hope my facial expression will do nothing to allay.

'Okay, so why didn't you show up?'

The violence of my outburst seems to surprise him. We face each other with suspicion. His is light, wary of being the butt of a secret joke, weighing gravity in one dark eye and mirth in the other, ready to laugh if the situation requires. Mine runs deeper.

'Pardon?'

I repeat myself, but louder this time so he can understand, a technique learned from Stephanie. My voice shakes.

A shadow passes over Noah's face as his mind sifts for the appropriate response. His eyes twitch from one side to the other, coming to rest intermittently on my face. Then he shrugs and the tension breaks.

'I'm sorry Rachel, I don't really know what you mean.'

I seek out the frayed cord that dangles from the front of my jacket, and twist it round my middle finger.

'All right. Twice we arrange to meet, and twice you don't turn up. And who is Jez White?'

'Jez White?' Noah frowns, relieved at the apparent change of subject, and at having a real question to consider. Although he would prefer one he can answer. 'I've no idea. Why?'

I help him out. 'The man who turns up instead of you whenever we arrange to meet? Your friend? Does that help?' Sarcasm has never been my forte. Tears have, however.

'Look, come and sit down and I'll warm up some tea.'

He is clearly rattled, and playing for time. I follow his lead to an area behind the rack of musty-smelling clothes where a single armchair sits battered and sagging next to a stove. I wonder if he sleeps here when the weather stops him getting home.

He disarms me of my umbrella and hooks it over the end of the rail, gesturing at me to sit. Calmed by the warmth of the stove, I struggle to keep my defences keen as I watch him swish the tea around in a pan, prolonging the silence, avoiding the conversation that must be continued whether he likes it or not.

He is shorter than I remember. But taller than White. The contours of his shoulder blades move in unison beneath his sweater, coming together then pulling apart again, like two bodies at play in the night. If memory serves.

It sounds stupid, but Jason is the only man I have ever slept with. Stephanie is not party to this information. He was the hypnotherapist who identified my recurring nightmares as premonitions. He took me on. The template of our sexual practice was drawn up the very first time we slept together, like an irreversible scientific formula. We approached each other as strangers would, in silence, in darkness, neither of us daring to look at the other's naked body. Jason would climb into bed first and lie there on his back, eyes shut, feigning sleep while I undressed with my back to him. When at last I slid in beside him he would stretch out an arm, eyes still closed, and roll me in towards him. We would lie there, our breathing affected, gentle fingers tapping at the skin of the other until at last we would kiss; the short tentative pecks of children. Our sex was fluid and seamless as in a dream. A serious affair. No laughter. No talking. We would doze off in languid motion, separate in sleep, and begin the next day as strangers once more. The times I have wondered how it would feel to sleep with another man, rubbed my own hands over my skin to emulate the touch of a stranger.

Noah's outstretched hand shakes as he passes me the tea. Nerves. Or the remnant of disease.

I take the bowl in both hands and blow onto the hot liquid. Noah drags a sack of beans closer to the stove and slumps onto it.

'How old are you?' I say.

'Thirty-four?'

'You look younger.'

'I might well be.'

We both smile. In truth neither of us is in a rush to rekindle our earlier discussion but it hangs between us, a void that cannot be filled with meaningless banter. Noah swigs his tea then makes the first move.

'So,' he says, measuring each word for accuracy, careful not to offend. 'You think you arrange to meet me, but when you get there someone else turns up who says he's a friend of mine?'

'Whoever I spoke to said they were you.'

'Did it sound like me? Where did you meet him?'

'I didn't really think about it. Edale the first time. Then Alderley Edge. He's got a big old car from before the burnouts. You must know him. Did you ever work at the solar plant?'

'Yes, for a bit.'

'Well, that's where he knows you from.'

Noah screws up his face and shrugs. 'I don't know who it could be. Plenty of people I know worked there. What does he look like?'

'Thin. Yellow hair. Mean eyes. Perhaps he comes in here.'

My portrayal rings no bells for Noah, but as I reel off my description an idea occurs to me. I keep it to myself for the time being.

'The thing is, Rachel,' he says, his tone more apologetic now but not quite riddled with the remorse I had hoped for. He thinks I am making it all up to manipulate him into spending time with me. 'The thing is, as I said before,

I hadn't even got round to calling you. To be honest, I lost your number the day you gave it to me.'

I turn the bowl round and round between my palms, creating miniature waves that lick at the rim and threaten to spill over.

Noah prattles on, something about knowing everyone in the area, but I have shut down, withdrawn, picked up and tiptoed away leaving an empty wax shell, that sits and stares into a bowl of tea to hold the fort in my absence. When I get home I'll call Stephanie and tell her the truth. I'll lose some ground but maybe she'll help me puzzle this out.

It is only when Noah calls out a greeting that I become aware of another presence in the market. I shrink lower in my chair. Without listening, I register the twittering tones of a young woman and the rustle of paper. Noah returns to his sack after an unusually rapid transaction.

'One of the New Dawners,' he says, with a wink.

Now I wish I had paid attention. I scrutinise his face, his smooth brown skin, wondering if he is trustworthy. If I trust him at all, choose to believe his version of events, then nothing that has happened makes any sense. I have never had the brain for puzzles. Jason was the logistical one, the clever one. Noah meets my gaze, and I am none the wiser. I elect to avoid the challenge altogether by reminding myself to check the blue bucket situation on the way home. If it has blown down I'll take it as a sign that events are working in my favour and Noah is telling the truth.

He has just repeated something for the third time. Hoping to summon a response. He seems pissed off, angry even. Time to go. It's clear he isn't prepared to help. I don't know if I can trust him and have no way of finding out. But I do have an idea that might force him to be straight with me and am keen to get home and put it into action. I unhook my umbrella from the rail.

'I'd best get going.'

Noah jumps to his feet. Over-animated in his relief, he slaps his pockets in search of his stubby pencil.

'Give me your number again,' he says, handing me a scrap of paper. 'If I come up with anything I'll call you.'

'No.'

If whoever it was that called me before should call again I will need to determine if it's Noah or an impostor. For now I will have to take him at his word.

'I'll come back when I've had time to think,' I say. I head for the door, and then stop. 'What's your mother's name?'

'She's dead. A long time since.'

'That doesn't matter.'

'Well, okay, if you say so. It's Zara.'

If whoever it is calls again, I can ask them that same question. If it is Noah he will give the right answer. Unless he is playing games with me, of course. At the very least I will know for certain if it isn't Noah. Or will I? I'm no good at this.

I take the long route home, nauseous with confusion, unable to focus on the questions never mind come up with any answers, but convinced of being the victim of someone's perverse entertainment. I pass the House of the New Dawn without breaking stride. The point of my umbrella scrapes a chalky trail on the road's surface behind me.

In the park, the blue bucket has fallen from the tree. Does that mean that Noah is telling the truth, or is a liar?

I don't remember. I scour the area round the tree's trunk, kicking at clumps of bracken and heaving belligerent swipes at the nettles with my umbrella. My search broadens in an ever-widening spiral until at last I have to admit defeat. Now the bucket has disappeared. Life is losing its simplicity.

That things are being tampered with, that this is a new game with as yet unfathomable rules, is clear. But beyond that is a huge, waterlogged knot that cannot be unravelled, and no amount of picking and pulling at it will lift my sense of unease. One small step out into the world and already I am in trouble. The pressure of living amongst others is upon me. The truth is, I don't much like other people, and here I am, being proved right again.

My toe stubs against a loose cobble. I kick it free from the mud and pick it up to measure the weight of it in both hands, rolling and tipping it from one hand to the other, in time with my footsteps. As I draw close to home, the wagon comes into view and my right arm, the arm holding the stone, raises, releases, lobs it at the windscreen. It bounces off, and when I move closer to inspect the damage I see it has left no more than a tiny spider's web of a scar. Disgusted at my own impotence, I turn away and climb the steps to the mill.

Still seething, I squat in front of the panel and begin to sketch; straight lines are impossible as the charcoal swerves over the uneven surface. These lines are just rough approximations of those stored in my memory, but I persevere, squinting with effort in the half-light, standing away at regular intervals and training the torch for a clearer view of my work. Jason's spirit hovers at my shoulder, taunting: *See, I bet that nose doesn't look the way you imagined it would.* I would turn now and smear my blackened fingers over his pristine features. Fuck off, Plato. Fuck off Jason. Fuck off Noah. Fuck off Jez fucking White. Fuck. Fucking. Off.

By nightfall the sketch is complete. A picture can be a thing of beauty even when its subject matter is not, which is the miracle of art. White. In black and white. Ha ha. I celebrate by preparing a meal of eggs and bread and settle down in the pale yellow gloom to eat my pale yellow food. My fingertips leave dusty black smudges on the bread as I use it to scoop up the egg.

Outside the wind squeals; it whistles at me through the shutter slats. The overhead light flickers and expires and candlelight throws long shapeless shadows across the walls. The effort of intense concentration has triggered a billowing headache behind my eyes. Tomorrow, if the light is good enough, I will attempt to paint. I survey the room, returning always to the same point, to the panel standing propped against the wall. His sketched outline dances in the blurring gloom. The chin is too narrow.

I take the panel by its corners and swivel it about, turn the picture to face the wall. My headache has spread to the base of my skull, and no amount of squeezing my eyes open and shut, or pressing at my brow bone, will weaken its grip. At last a dark sleep takes me.

The morning is calm. Shielding my eyes from the thin morning glare, I look up at the flat silver sky. A good light for painting.

Although my palette is restricted to colours made from grass, earth, and my own dried blood, it will suffice to recreate a head dyed red by firelight and eyes green with deception. I crack on.

Rain has started up a polite, irregular tapping at the windows, as if trying to go about its business without disturbing my concentration; warning me the light will soon be gone. Gnawing the wooden point of my paintbrush between my front teeth until its frayed end resembles the brush end's sickly twin, I cast my mind back to that night in the Nag's Head; to his features etched into my brain tissue. It takes no time to capture the essence of his blank green stare; his narrow, unkind mouth. No one could fail to recognise him.

I close the window against the burgeoning downpour. Satisfied with my efforts at last, I search for a new purpose to bide the time it takes for the painting to dry, a task, something other than sleeping.

In the bedroom, a single drop of water rolls across the ceiling; too weak or too lazy to complete the journey to the other side, it peels away and drops onto the bed; one of the reasons I don't sleep here too often, and why the blue bucket would have come in handy. It is followed by another, and then another, hatching in quicker and quicker succession until the dripping becomes a trickle.

Access to the attic is through a hole in the bathroom ceiling. I clamber first onto the side of the bath, get my balance, then reach up to grab the sides of the hole while stepping up onto the edge of the basin. From there, I poke my head up into the loft and strain my ears to identify the singular pop of water falling onto hardboard.

I haul myself up and crawl above the bedroom, patting the floor in search of a damp patch. Just as I am about to give up, a hard, cold droplet hits the crown of my head. Guessing where it would have landed if my head hadn't been in the way, I mark the spot with one hand and roll onto my side to stretch for the bucket with the other. In theory I would measure the interval between drips to estimate how long the bucket will take to fill up, but already the rain is easing; the drip has become lazy, and so have I. With the bucket in place, I climb back down to the bathroom.

I check the view from the bedroom window, half expecting to see the return of the stranger. Nothing and no one is there, but a single great soft white flake rides an unseen current like a delirious fairy. Snow. It dithers towards the river below as if aware of its fate. What use is such precise individuality when faced with imminent dissolution?

Snow can lift my heart in a way that sunshine never could. I run downstairs, pull on my outdoor things, and rush out into the yard. Snowflakes catch on my eyelashes and tingle soft against my cheek. I look for a job that will keep me outdoors.

All that remains of the log pile are a few chunks of apple wood; as good for burning as a pile of wet leaves, useful only for filling the house with sweet-smelling smoke and therefore not useful at all.

I load the axe into the wheelbarrow and manoeuvre it out into the yard. The cold of the handles penetrates the loose knit of my gloves, stinging my hands. The axe bangs out a jumble of rhythms as we go, drums a half-remembered melody into my head that goes in one ear and out the other. I don't know when there stopped being music.

I steer the barrow through the yard gate, scraping the sides, metal against metal, bringing the axe-music to a teeth-grating crescendo. Out in the lane the wagon lies on its side, fallen victim to the storm. Snow settles on its tyres like petals thrown into an open grave. I'm better off without it, wish it good riddance and point the barrow so that its front wheel dredges a furrow in the slush towards the park.

I don't have to go far. Just beyond the gate an oak tree has keeled over, its roots waterlogged and rotting, and is leaning against the wall. Just above head height dangles an otherwise healthy limb that has been lopped by the storm. The bark at its joint has been stripped away to expose pulp the colour of flesh in a child's painting. The game now is to jump and catch the lower end of the branch. This one I'm good at.

My first attempt fails, the branch springs out of my grasp, snagging my gloves and grazing the flesh beneath, and I drop knee-deep into brackish water, but on my second jump I manage to grab it with both hands, my arms stretched almost out of their sockets. Bearing down with all my weight, I swing from side to side, knees bent, feet off the ground. The twisting action works at the strip of connecting bark until the branch rips completely away. It's a big one. I avoid being hit by jumping to one side, and then pat the tree by way of thanks, as you would an elephant that has returned you safely to earth with its trunk.

I drag the branch onto the path and strip it of twigs for use as kindling. Pinning it to the ground with my left foot, I raise the axe two-handed, bring it around in a wide swoop, and in one movement split the green bark. Sweat sticks and unsticks the skin under my breasts as I pick my way across to the thin end of the branch. Rhythm is the key to chopping wood; without rhythm it takes twice the effort. Jason would sing to keep time, loud and tuneless, but with a passion to break a heart. I offer the occasional grunt. I roll the remaining section of branch with my foot. Three more and I am done and at last I can straighten my aching back. It has stopped snowing.

A final burst of yellow light stains the western sky where a sunset might once have promised a fine day to follow. I toss the logs one by one over the stile, collect the kindling into a bundle, climb over, and load the barrow.

13.9.43

She is upset, my sweet Paloma. She believes he has tricked her and that is good. Now we have met I can see to it that she will soon give up on him. And although she seems not to care and teases me without mercy, things are going to plan. But I refuse to chase. The wild can be tamed and power can be taken by force. True strength and dignity is in waiting. She must believe she has earned my protection and love. Fly to me, my tantalising dove. I am ready for you.

It is her hand on me. Stroking. Her mouth takes me.

9.56pm. full orgasm. missionary.

Dawn lurks behind the shutters, a long-anticipated visitor waiting to be invited in, but for now it must stay where it is, for I am eager to be on my way.

The panel is heavy and awkward to carry and it will take me much longer than usual to walk to the market. The wagon would be useful now, but I try not to think about that. What's gone is gone, and anyway it would have made me too conspicuous.

The early morning is cold but dry, and the pale sky to the east suggests a good chance of its staying that way for a while. I hold the painting against my chest like an oversized shield, lifting my chin so as not to scrape it on the rough edge. As I turn into the road, the icy northeasterly presses it to me so that its bottom edge bangs my knees, reducing my stride to quick, short, teetering steps.

When at last I arrive, the market is closed. I hammer at the door in case Noah is locked inside, asleep in the chair, but to no avail. I could cry. It never occurred to me that he might not be here.

I lug the panel back through the precinct to my doorway, to shelter from the wind until he turns up. Even the ginger cat has abandoned its post. I remove my hard hat, put up my hood, swaddle myself in my coat and settle down to wait. It is beginning to bother me that I need so much sleep. As soon as my body stops moving, no matter if it is day or night, I drop off. A wash of tiredness comes over me now and I have to stand up and do a little jig in the narrow confines of the doorway to keep myself awake.

'Hello!'

It's Noah. I stop dancing.

'Keeping warm?'

'Yes.'

'You're up and about early today.'

'Are you open now?'

'Oh, yes.'

I pick up the panel.

'Aha. Not seen one of these for a long time.' He attempts to peer over my shoulder. 'Let's have a look, then.'

I step aside in a matador's pose to show him my work, twisting my neck to get a glimpse of his immediate impression, but his face shows no glimmer of recognition.

'It's very good,' he says. 'Be a shame to trade it up.'

'It's not staying. Do you think it's a good likeness?'

'Mmm. Who of? Is it a self-portrait?'

I allow a little longer for the dawn of recognition to break, but he still doesn't get it, or pretends not to.

'It's him,' I say at last. I turn to look at Noah face on, to enjoy his discomfort eye to eye.

'Who?' he asks again. 'I'm sorry, I'm no good at guessing games.'

'Jez White,' I say. 'Your friend.'

Noah inspects the painting, a look of horror on his face.

'Would you like some breakfast?' His tone is altered, kinder. He feels sorry for me. 'It's bubble and squeak.'

'I don't know what that is.'

'Tatties, basically. Fried. With cabbage as a rule, but I don't have any. So I suppose it's just the bubble, or the squeak, I'm not sure which. I'll put an onion in it to tart it up.' A pause. 'Look, Rachel, I promise you I have no idea who this person is. It's a great painting, though. Come on.'

He picks up the panel and carries it through the precinct and into the market. I tag along like an idiot child as he leads me through to the back of the shop, where I hover next to the clothes rail. Noah points at the chair and, obedient dog that I am, I sit.

My mouth floods with saliva at the smell of frying potatoes. I take the proffered bowl in both hands, warming them on its rough surface. Noah seats himself on his favourite sack and uses dirty fingers to throw lumps of potato into his open mouth. My own fingers fiddle with the contents of my bowl.

'Tuck in,' he says.

Nothing I make is ever this delicious. But Noah was a Traveller, was born into this life, has probably had things much harder; he knows how to do things.

I notice him staring at the painting.

'So do you not even recognise him as someone who comes in here?' I say.

'That's what I was wondering,' he says, 'but I really have no idea. He has very green eyes. I'm sure I'd remember those. Have there been any more phone calls?'

'No.'

'How come you're so keen to find him, then? Do you like him?' He is teasing me. And without a hint of jealousy, which pisses me off.

'No, of course not. He's the ugliest man I've ever met. It's something to do, I suppose,' is all I say. Then, to prove my point, I rise and turn the painting to the wall. I return to my seat and stuff the last few lumps of potato into my mouth, then speak again.

'Where do you live?'

A starchy white blob ejects from my mouth as I speak and lands in my lap. He pretends not to notice.

'In a community house, over by Lymm.'

Of course, he would live in a community.

'Quite near me then,' I say. We could be friends if it weren't for this business with White.

'Not far. I see you sometimes, when I'm out on my travels.' Then he stands. He has talked long enough and there is work to be done.

'Have you shown your painting to anyone else?' He keeps his voice casual.

'No, I haven't. Can I take some soya beans with me?'

'Yes, of course, but you're not going out in this weather. The wind'll skin you alive. The New Dawners brought some books in the other day. Can you read?'

He drags a small wooden crate over to my feet. The books are swollen with water damage, their pages spread into a fan.

'Help yourself,' he says. 'And help yourself to some tea if you want.'

I am not convinced of a dramatic change in the weather. It always sounds worse inside the market, the wind screeches through the precinct like a banshee, but I select a book at random, read the title out loud, *The Handmaid's Tale*, and open it midway. Maybe his plan is for us to be stranded here together.

I decide to stay long enough to convince him of my trust, to show him I can relax in his presence, then I'll make up an excuse to leave.

Holding the book so close to my face that individual letters blur together like a trail of squashed ants, I sniff the sweet smell of old paper and pretend to immerse myself in words, so that he won't expect me to talk; but I am struggling under the weight of disappointment. Nothing is turning out as I hoped. The secret of White's identity is still a mystery and an ever more compelling one. In a few breaths I am asleep, drugged by the warmth of the stove and, although I would never admit to such a thing, sedated by the simple presence of another human being.

When I come to, the weather really has worsened, but despite Noah's concerns I insist on setting out for home. He tries but fails to persuade me to at least leave the painting behind for collection another day, but the truth is, I have had another idea and am keen to put it into action. Noah insists on binding the panel to my back with rope, which is easier but forces me to walk bent over like a crone. I stop in the doorway and try to look back at him.

'Do you know what the time is?'

'The time? No idea. It's very hard to tell in this weather. Why?'

'Nothing. I'd best be off. Thanks for breakfast.'

With the panel on my back and the wind behind me, I am forced to walk at a faster pace than I have the energy for. Falling debris taps out little tunes on my hard hat and I march along in time, or imagine that I do. A fine young conifer has been blown across the road in the exact place that the dead fox occupied. I sidle around it and make a mental note never to stop for long in that spot.

By the time the back of the New Dawn house comes grey and cheerless into view, I need a rest, as I predicted I would. I'm thinking now that if there are men in there, as

Noah seems to believe, then White could be one of them, and it is entirely feasible that the New Dawners know as much about Noah as he does about them, if not more; gossip backfires.

I duck into the porch and release the panel from my back. It drops to the ground with a crack and I lean it against the porch frame. My hand hovers in mid-air above the knocker. Suppose he does live here? It occurs to me that I have not accounted for actually finding him, especially with so little effort. For all I know he could be a being from a parallel universe, a living breathing ghost, or a figment of my imagination, invented in a series of storm-induced dreams to appease a solitary existence. It's possible. In truth I have no expectation of ever finding him, and no real desire to do so. I'm simply enjoying the search.

I appeal to the whipping wind for courage, lift the brass knocker and shrink back as it thuds against the door. A rustle from the other side, a lowered voice, and the door swings inward. A candle. A rosy face. A smile.

'My! How are you? Come in, come in.'

She seems to know me, to be expecting me, almost. Her hand touches my sleeve and I am led into a cavernous hallway, its size indeterminate beyond the candle's halo.

'Generador's oud again.'

Apologetic and smiling. A strange muddle of an accent. Like Stephanie with a permanent head cold.

'Boy, is she raving oud there today! Come through, come through.'

My guide – she has that air about her – leads the way, her glistening white head a beacon in the candlelight. A thick plait stretches the length of her back like an external spine, silver against the azure of her long shift. A pre-Raphaelite queen. Few women are born so gorgeous. She was born to be followed and I would follow her anywhere, my booted feet clumsy in the wake of her ethereal grace.

The wind, as it worries the corners of the house, imitates the low voices of whispering spies that seem to come from the landing above. The woman stops, her hand resting on the handle of a heavy wooden door, and turns towards me. In no way are her features made sinister by the candle's uplight but I am reminded of my painting, outside in the porch.

'Id is warmest in here,' she says.

She pulls at the door and a triangle of orange light cuts a swathe in the floor. She beckons to me to follow her through.

'The kitchen.' She introduces me to the empty room.

At least one third of the far wall is taken up with a fireplace, ablaze with more logs than I could gather in a whole day, its hearth fringed by a row of tiny candles, their flames shrunken and cringing in deference to the great furnace behind. An oak table runs the length of the room, flanked by numerous stools and high-backed chairs, its polished surface liquid in the firelight. A tall iron candlestick forms the table's centrepiece.

'Please, take off your coad and boods and make yourself comfortable.' She places a small round cushion on the seat of a chair and pulls the chair closer to the fire. 'I am Momma.'

Her three short words are imbued with finality, as if they contain all the information I will ever need. The end of the line. The ultimate affirmation. I am Momma. I am Momma. Iammomma. A mantra for the faint of heart, the hunted, the lost. Momma. It reverberates round the room, levelling my breath, catching up my thoughts in a mesh to keep them safe until later.

I do as she says, remove my jacket, hang it over the ladderback of the chair, and sit down. A plate, bowl and cup, the same stuff they trade at the market, land silently on the table at my side.

'You must be tired?'

No, I have to remind myself, I am not. I slept at the market. But yet I feel drowsy, intoxicated. Hypnotised.

'Id's the wind, she can drain it righd oud of you,' Momma whispers. 'Are you on your way home?'

I rouse myself. 'I've been to the market, to show Noah my painting.'

Momma's face has the ability to form a question without any flicker of a muscle.

'I'm a painter. He likes to see my work,' I say.

It will be difficult to lie to Momma. With her there is no need to lie. If I lie, the fire will put out a great tongue and set light to my hair. It is equally impossible to ask her anything.

'Did you leave id with him?' Momma's eyes are round and deep, like a baby's.

'I left it out in the porch. If you like I can show it to you when I leave?'

I am a child, eager to show off my latest masterpiece to an indifferent parent. Momma rises. 'Please ead.' She glides towards the door and leaves the room.

Has she gone to fetch my painting, or to look at it? I await the gust of cold air that will herald her return and contemplate the simple meal before me: a bowl of steaming brown soup, a perfectly round knob of grey bread, a triangle of white cheese, and a square of yellow butter. A child's play-set of a meal. It would be rude not to eat it. I am the ginger cat, and Momma is me. The knife flicks its reflection across the ceiling when I pick it up.

I turn my chair in to the table and eat slowly, casting surreptitious glances at the door as I chew and slurp, sweating in the heat of the fire at my back, but not daring to change places.

I listen for evidence of movement from the house's inhabitants. The wind plays about the chimney like a dragon's breath, its roiling as familiar as my own heartbeat but for the high-pitched overtone that weaves in and out of the swirling. I listen harder. A sharp-edged screech cuts through the turmoil, and then vanishes. A woman in pain. Excruciating pain.

Careful not to make a sound, I stand. My hands are trembling, probably from the heat, as I lift my jacket from the back of the chair and put it on; its fabric is hot and sticky from being too close to the fire. I slip away from the table, my ears alert to every murmur.

The hall is quiet. I stop in the open doorway long enough for my eyes to readjust to the gloom, using the light from the kitchen to memorise my route to the front door. I rush forward, eyes fixed in the direction I have to go, my body following the lead of my own stare as a horse's would.

'I'm sorry to have left you. One of our sisders is in labour.' Momma's voice interrupts my flight. I turn to see a silver Momma-shaped aura floating above the staircase.

'The wind is still fierce. Are you sure you'll be all righd?'

'Oh, yes, I'll be fine, thank you. I have a hard hat.' I tug at the door, but not hard enough to open it first time.

'Well, do come and visid again soon. Id is good to see you.'

Like an old friend. Or mother.

'You'll forgive me for nod coming down. I really oughda ged back to the baby.' Old-fashioned manners, familiar and formal.

'Of course.' The only possible answer. I am starting to remember how people speak to each other, or how they used to speak to each other. I look up one last time; Momma has vanished.

I stand in the porch and strap on my hard hat. I will go anyway, despite the gale. If I can bind it on without help, the panel will protect my back.

I turn its painted side towards me. I turn it away again. Both sides are blank. A few dirty smudges are all that remain of the portrait. A million tiny scratches score the gesso as if the image has been scrubbed away with wire wool. All that remains is a faint green circle, the glimmer of a retreating eye. Queasy with confusion, I scan the air for some trace of White's face being whisked away on the breeze. But this is an attack on me, not him. I struggle to fix the panel onto my back, more determined now than ever not to leave it behind.

I take a risk and cut through the park to shorten the journey home, and try not to think about who might have committed such a malevolent act. I have trained myself not to think too much because thinking only dredges up the past, but am aware that I may have to untrain myself.

Eyes open, eyes shut, it makes no difference. My saliva tastes of earth and blood. I am lying face down in pitch darkness. I attempt to push myself up onto my hands but my arms are weak and something is weighing heavily on my back, holding me under. My neck is fixed into position, twisted to one side. A pinprick of consciousness steals over my body like a probe, activating pain wherever it touches a joint. My neck burns when I move my head.

Shaking with cold and shock, I bend my arms behind me to fumble with the rope that is still wound round my middle, and work it loose enough to allow me to slither out from under the panel. I push the panel to one side and heave myself onto all fours. My right ankle will take no weight but for the moment is not painful. I sit back onto the panel. My fall has made a nest of the bracken and nettles, my legs, face and hands are peppered with stings.

The weather has calmed but I have missed the transition from day to night. Keen to locate my whereabouts, I listen for the distant hiss of the weir. I can just make out the silhouette of the stone lion that guards the entrance to the mansion house, which means I am not far from home, but I have no strength now to carry the panel; it will be safe where it is, under the tree, until I am able to fetch it.

By raking the bracken with my good foot I seek out my umbrella, check its stem is intact, then commit my weight to it and hobble homewards.

As a young girl I liked to venture into the quietest darkest places at night, in search of fear. But the dark never scared me; it would wrap itself round me like the arm of an old friend. The more I sought to scare myself, the more protected I felt. Things are changing.

All is quiet but for the shaky rise and fall of my breath. In an effort to stimulate my circulation I imagine myself in a fiery orange room. But it's all too much.

14.9.43

Her dumb ignorance has put me, and our chances of being together, in grave danger. If she has so much as thought my name in Momma's presence I have had it. I have no choice for now but to lie low and trust that our bond and her desire will bring her to me.

If you love something, let it go.

8.50pm. ¹/₂ orgasm. standing.

Stiff fingers uncurl and massage through clumps of matted hair until they encounter a lump the size of an egg. So much for my hard hat. The gentle pressure aggravates a surface bruising but no deeper pain. An empty protest. I shift onto my back.

Someone scrubbed out my painting, I remember that much. And did that same person then try to kill me? Momma and Noah would not be the first people I have met whose immense outer beauty harbours an essential evil, and I doubt they will be the last. Only Noah saw the painting of White for certain, although Momma, or anyone else at the New Dawn house for that matter, maybe even White himself, could have seen it.

Too dazed to curb my rising levels of paranoia any other way, I heave myself up and pat at the covers in search of the phone. The line connects and the gentle purr of the ringing tone soothes me, but Stephanie doesn't answer.

I am still dressed for the outdoors, boots and all. I loosen the strings of my right boot and prise it as wide apart as it will go to slide my foot out without too much aggravation. My ankle is swollen and the colour of a dying hydrangea; the slightest movement is agony. Using my umbrella as a crutch, I hop through to the kitchen. Eating is a good cure for trauma.

Compared to the golden warmth of Momma's kitchen, the light in my own is cold and brittle. Working with my elbows resting on the counter for support, I dislodge a lump of red lentils from the bottom of their container. I tease them apart by rinsing them in the stream of tap water and throw them into the pot with a chopped potato and some water.

The stove is out and the new logs are all outside and probably still wet, so I resort for the first time to the electric hob that Jason installed for use in emergencies. Not being able to walk surely constitutes an emergency. The lights dim when I plug it in but it works all right.

I open the window and sniff at the hogweed-scented air, try to determine which end of the night it is. Night into day or day into night. My hand slides again over the bump on my head, traces the altered contours of my skull. I shut the window. A murky scum is frothing the surface of the thickening soup. I stir it in, more for my own comfort than for any culinary advantage.

For someone who predicted the fate of a whole planet, I am amazed at my own incompetence when it comes to the control of my own microcosmic corner of it. Afflicted by an acute hyperopia I am useless with detail; I can function in the day to day only by imagining what someone else, Jason or Stephanie, would do in any given situation, and then act according to that assumption. I know exactly what Jason would do at this point: he would indulge in some *forward thinking*: human life has been all but eradicated through short-sightedness, he would say. That man could fit anything into a nutshell.

But knowing what I would or should do is a whole other matter.

In practice, Jason's forward thinking involved the pinning of scraps of paper covered in lists to every available blank surface in the house. Jason loved lists. He would make lists of things he had already done just for the pleasure of crossing them out. Pointless. But in this time of crisis I cannot afford to sneer at any method that might help me build a winning strategy. I am at war with an unknown enemy and I have to start somewhere.

I leave off my stirring and go in search of a pencil. The last remaining blank page at the back of my beloved *Woyzeck* is the only clean sheet of paper that remains outside of Jason's study, which is out of bounds, and therefore must be sacrificed to a higher cause. I rip the page away from its seam, taking care not to loosen the corresponding printed page at the front of the book, and begin by listing all the things I need to make a list of:

1. *Unusual things that have happened*
2. *Things to do*
3. *Places to go*

My fingers are so stiff I can barely grip the pencil, and I wish I knew the whereabouts of my glasses.

I draw three straightish columns, the pencil wobbling over the grain of the table beneath the paper, and head up each one with an item from the list. Under *Places to go* I write the sub-heading *(T=Trustworthy/U=Untrustworthy)*; below that I write three names:

Noah (?)
Momma/New Dawn (U)
Jez White (U)

So far I have established that there is no one I can trust. I knew that already.

Under *Things to do* I write:

> *visit Noah (✓)*
> *paint White (✓)*
> *find White*

Already I glimpse the immense satisfaction to be had from ticking off already completed tasks.

The third column poses a problem. How far into the past should I go? Life has been a stream of unusual events as far back as I can remember. Perhaps begin with Jason's departure. I write it in and immediately cross it out again. I don't have enough paper to go that far back. I need to focus on the present dilemma. The disappearance of the dead fox on the day I propositioned Noah is as good a marker as any, so I begin there:

> *dead fox*
> *person by water mill?*
> *man on canal path*
> *White*
> *bucket*
> *painting*
> *accident (?) in park*

I experience an unexpected rush of achievement. This is more than just forward thinking; it shows the makings of a project. As the mill was Jason's project, as I myself was Jason's project, this one is mine. Self-interest alone persuades me to hold on to this seed of a mystery, to nurture it as a potential source of entertainment. My eyes fix on the crucial words: *find White*. What I will do if I find him remains undecided. Follow him? Befriend him? Seduce him? Paint him again? The possible outcomes are infinite; they fan out into such a rainbow of potential that even if I never find him, the anticipation of finding him, the search itself, could keep me occupied for months, if not years. Good projects like this are not easily come by.

Adrenalin flushes through my system, eases my throbbing ankle, heightens my senses, alerts me to the aroma of stewing lentils wafting through from the kitchen. I go back to my stirring.

The soup has turned to sludge and is sticking to the bottom of the pan, but the lentils are still gritty and uncooked. I pour more water on, stir it in, and then ladle some out into a bowl. A lump of hard bread completes the meal. It is not quite up to New Dawn standards but it will do.

The western sky, instead of lightening, has turned a deep aubergine as another storm moves in off the Atlantic. As I eat, a cloud the size of Warrington unloads a ton of hailstones onto the mill, the park and the golf course; it is God throwing all the lost golf balls back to earth, thirty years too late.

I put down my spoon and look out of the window. The scene has reversed. The sky over the canal path is now clear while the sky beyond the park and to the east is dark as night, as if the house has turned on a 180-degree axis while I was eating.

I take a cloth from the kitchen and bump down the stairs on my bottom, a useful technique remembered from childhood. Then I hop outside to demolish one of the icy pyramids that have collected in the corners of the courtyard. I wrap enough hailstones in the cloth to make a cold compress for my ankle.

Back inside, I clear a space on the living room floor and lie down in it with the ice pack pressed to my swollen foot.

The chill of inertia tingles between my shoulder blades. My body is heavy and numb. I roll onto my side, into the puddle of melted ice at my feet. For a moment I think the floods have come and the shock of it jolts me awake and projects me bolt upright. I regain my composure, take up the sopping cloth, drip it through to the kitchen and slop it into the sink.

I need to speak to Stephanie, to set the record straight and work out where to go from here.

I try the phone again, but it is more than dead. Even when the lines are out there is always static, but when I press the connect button this time it triggers nothing, just ominous dead air. I try the radio; if the radio is working there can't be anything seriously wrong. Nothing. I crank the handle to its point of resistance. Again nothing, just the whirr of the radio's internal mechanism, picking up no signal. I've always known this would happen eventually.

I'm on my own, and I have a job to do. I must go about things more methodically. White may well be at the New Dawn house but it may be easier to track him down by process of elimination and so I shouldn't discount the other communities; if I'm to find him I'm going to have to overcome my social reticence.

I alter my chart, writing under *Places to go*:

Home Farm
New Dawn
Foxleyhall
Noah's community

Home Farm will be my first stop.

Home Farm is a small community lying to the southeast of the park, closest to the mill, and the oldest in the area. It was Jason's performance there that set him up as community linchpin. Its establishment coincided with our beginning to argue about babies.

'I want a baby,' I would say. Kept on saying. *Ad infinitum*.

Jason would jam his lips together and force himself to speak through them.

'Not again, Rachel. Please.'

I would be crying and all he would do was stare at me, his eyes wide and blank. The delusion of détente that we had been living under for a while had offered us some measure of comfort, but it was being chipped away at by my shameless and unreasonable desire to drag an innocent being into this world without hope.

I couldn't win. Jason said he had risked everything for me, tied himself to the tracks of public ridicule to appease my dystopian vision of the future and now I wanted to move the goalposts. Selfish bitch, couldn't let anything rest.

'Why don't you look at what's going on around us, Rachel?'

'You tell me, what is going on around us, Jason? I can't see a fucking thing over that wall of yours.'

'Of *mine*?'

'I'm thirty-six years of age and I want a baby. You're always telling me to behave more normally. What's more normal than wanting a baby at thirty-six?'

He stood up, shaking his head.

'Where are you going?'

'Out!'

Because now, he had somewhere else to go. But as soon as his foot hit the bottom stair, he would swivel about and march back up again, by which time I would be lying on the sofa with my back to the room. To him.

'What about typhoid then – how do you envisage protecting a baby against that. Eh?' (Prod.) 'Or malaria. Or any one of these mystery viruses that just come out of nowhere. It's not safe, Rachel.' He would be shouting, out of control. It was as if someone had pulled the plug on a bath full of putrid stagnant water, and from the way he would clutch at his belly when we fought, its vortex seemed to be located somewhere in the region of his navel.

'How about the same way we protect ourselves?' I would mumble into the sofa. 'How do other people do it? Other people must be having babies.'

'No, Rachel, they are not. Not healthy ones anyway. Have you looked at the river lately? They don't even bother to wrap the bodies any more, and they only expend precious energy on throwing them in there in the hope they won't be fished out and eaten by some other starving bastard. Open the window – what can you smell? Roses? How can you be so fucking selfish?' He would turn again to leave. Lecture over? Not yet. He couldn't resist, couldn't let it go, had to urge those last grey dregs towards the plughole, using his hands if necessary. His voice would take on a wavering monotone. 'You cannot live for years crying Apocalypse, and then, when it comes, decide that all is well with the world after all, just because it suits *you*!'

I would make a show of covering my ears, but had no real defence against his argument. How I despised his lisping sanctimony, and especially the exaggerated calm with which he pulled on the door into the mill. Off he would go to play guru and disciple with his gang of devotees at Home Farm.

From the window I would watch him climb the stile into the park. It was his habit after one of these episodes to seat himself on the top rung and look back towards the mill, towards the river, sluggish and thick in the drought, and to run through the argument once more in his head, to check the detail of it and to justify his position.

People were dying because they no longer knew how to survive. People were killing each other over the possession of a shrivelled potato or a sip of polluted water. People were killing each other out of mercy, while they still had the energy to do it, because heat and disease, those omnipresent vultures, rode your shoulder, picked at your living flesh. Thousands, maybe millions, there was no way of knowing, had already died, of malaria, typhoid, starvation, heatstroke, hypothermia; of fear, violence, confusion. The infrastructure, the illusory safety net upon which life had become so dependent, had collapsed.

As he stared back at the mill, he would survey the turbine, which at that time was still waiting, in all its supercilious glory, for the weather to change; at the water filters, which had still to experience their first downpour. I was a foetus, encased in the storm wall's womb, waiting to be born.

He couldn't understand why I wasn't grateful. We were ahead of the game. Almost safe.

Then he would straighten his back and release a tiny pool of sweat from the creases in his midriff, to spill over his navel and soak into the waistband of his shorts. Climbing down into the park to continue the short walk to Home Farm, he could breathe more easily in the shade of the trees, whose scorched leaves would soon drop from exhaustion.

Home Farm had been squatted by a small group of Travellers; forced out of their vehicles by fuel shortages and burnouts, they found shelter in abandoned buildings. Jason was helping them to build water tanks and a makeshift turbine. Together they planted a semicircle of conifers around what Jason predicted would be the most vulnerable aspect of the farmhouse. He had their trust, and in return they offered him friendship and sanity. Community. He was soon in demand, with requests for help arriving daily from similar groups all across the district and beyond. It was as if once the mill was finished he forgot that the vision that had made it all possible was mine; he had adopted it, sold it as his own, and become king of the community dwellers. He got it right. *I* got it right. He took all the glory, while I became invalid, in every sense of the word. I hated him for that.

When I arrive, the gate at the end of the Home Farm drive is shut but low enough to climb over. A panting black and white dog eyes me through the bars. I know this dog, we have met many times in the park, but he may be less friendly on his own territory. I twist my hand through the bars towards his nose. He sniffs my fingertips then swipes at them with his steaming pink tongue.

His panting, smiling attitude holds as I lift myself onto the middle bar of the gate and swing a leg over the top. Not quite up to the standard of Jason's gate vaults, but he is impressed. He jumps up at me, frustrated little whimpering noises squirrelling in his throat.

I drop to the ground, and he is off, bounding towards the house. He turns back to check I am following, then lollops off again. He comes back and runs in circles round me then stops in my path, waiting, front paws stretched out, arse in the air, tongue dripping sideways. I almost catch him up; he runs off again barking and disappears round the side of the house. I don't follow.

The front of the house faces east but as it's down in a dip I doubt it would ever have seen the sun rise. It is square and built of red brick, its windows evenly spaced, open and friendly, with its face half hidden under green-black and apple-red creepers. A handsome house. Jason's neat semicircle of conifers stand at a safe distance, their stunted brown tops disturbed by the breeze.

A yap breaks the peace, and the dog reappears, trotting close at the heels of a young woman, who smiles and waves a gloved hand as she picks her way through the mud. Her sleeves are rolled up showing one arm to be bandaged. Anxious to keep her at a distance, I call over as soon as she is close enough to hear.

'I've a message for Jez.'

'Hello,' the woman calls back. 'I didn't recognise you at first. You're Rachel, aren't you? From the mill?'

She points in the direction of the park, just in case I don't know where my own house is. People are stupid.

'Yes.'

I have never met this woman but, like Momma, she seems to know who I am. Perhaps this isn't such a good idea. I skip the pleasantries.

'Is there someone here called Jez? I've a message for him.'

The woman takes a step closer, and I step backwards. She stops and we continue to shout across to each other. The dog scampers backwards and forwards in the mud between us, as if translating our exchange into paw prints.

'A message? For Jed?'

'Jez.' I emphasise the zed at the end. Perhaps she's deaf as well as stupid. 'Blond hair. My height.'

The woman screws up her eyes and shakes her head.

'We've a Jed, but he's dark. Have you asked down at the market?'

'Yes, but maybe he thought I said Jed too. Never mind, it's not important.' I back away, keen to escape.

'Would you like some tea?'

'No, thanks. It's very kind of you, but I'd best be off.'

'All right then, if you're sure, I'll get back to my digging. It's nice to see you again. Call in any time.'

She turns back the way she came. I head up the drive with the dog at my heels. He is calmer now, sensitive perhaps to my disappointment. The woman calls after me, 'Any news of Jason?'

I pretend not to hear her over the mud-sucking slurp of my footsteps, over the panting of the dog, over the sighing of the wind in the conifers. I too can be hard of hearing.

The dog waits until I have climbed the gate, then cocks his leg and pees against the gatepost before he turns to run home. I set off in the direction of the New Dawn house.

The woman who answers the door is a less stunning version of Momma. A generation younger and dressed in grey drab.

'I would like to see Momma,' I say.

'Is she expecting you?'

Her voice is timid, less ripe than Momma's.

'No, not exactly.'

'Please remove your boots. May I take your name?'

'It's Rachel.'

The already grey border at the hem of my skirt has soaked up the fresh mud and spread to knee level. My face burns with embarrassment as I fumble with my boot strings. Momma let me keep them on. I wish I had made this my first call so I would at least have been cleaner. Deputy Momma waits while I prise the strings apart and set my boots side by side in the porch. Too intimidated to ask if I can bring them indoors in case of theft, I leave it to chance.

The giant checkerboard floor is lit by daylight filtered through a huge window halfway up the stairs. Otherwise the hallway is as devoid of life as before. I follow the woman through to the kitchen. The contrast between the hall and the kitchen is as marked as the difference between the winters and summers of my childhood.

The woman sweeps over to the stove, gesturing at the table as she passes. I sit in the same chair as before and no sooner am I seated than I am presented with a bowl and plate, also as before, although this time its delivery lacks a certain grace and the bowl contains tea, not soup. I decide they have a cupboard full of these snacks, ready prepared for the satisfaction of a constant stream of visitors.

'Thank you,' I say.

My attendant nods a bow in the style of Momma then glides out of the room. I peer at the hem of her skirt as she departs, hoping to catch a glimpse of a foot, proof of mortal status. Has she gone to fetch Momma, or has my request been misinterpreted as an excuse to come in and be fed? I sit, watching the door, nibbling and listening. I am beginning to forget how hunger feels.

The tea Noah made me was male and intricate, but dependent on nettles for its predominant flavour, while the tea of the New Dawn is simple and delicate, the most delicious I have ever tasted, scented with roses and apples, and a mystery ingredient that also perfumes the candles they trade at the market. I try to identify it as I sip, but fail, which is probably for the best.

I lick my index finger and dab at the table, pick up stray crumbs and flick them onto my plate. For a house containing a new baby, the peace is alarming. An appalling thought strikes me. What if the baby died? I may be intruding on a period of mourning. I dare myself to risk refilling my bowl. I am helping myself to the contents of a wooden ladle when the click of the door alerts me to the woman's return. I blush with guilt but the woman shows no sign of disapproval. Instead she slides in between table and bench and sits down.

'Momma is very sorry, she is unable to see you today, but please stay and finish your tea.'

Her delivery is now sweet and chirrupy, as if Momma is speaking through her. I return to my place at the table and glance across at my companion. I want to ask about the baby, but she sits, head lowered, hands locked together on the table in the same way that Jason sometimes would before he ate. Other times he would hover them, palms flat, just above his food, his eyes shut. Wanker.

'You may be able to help me anyway?'

The woman raises her head out of respect for the fact that I have spoken. Had she forgotten I was here?

'I'm looking for someone. A man. I think his name is Jez White. Does he live here?'

The woman chews on some invisible thing, her jaws sliding across one another in a slow rhythm, clicking once on each turn. She swallows.

'I am not party to that information, I'm afraid. You will have to ask Momma.' She pauses a moment. 'Momma says you are welcome to call back another time.' A smile.

Her blackened teeth undermine her serenity. She is almost normal. I am peeved that they have sent someone so lowly to deal with me, but I manage to smile back at her; I am getting nowhere. My bowl is empty now but for a few specks of indeterminate foliage floating in a spoonful of tea. It would be impossible to swig the final mouthful without swallowing the dregs. Time to go.

I stand in the porch looking out, listening, and half expecting to hear the house erupt into raucous life with relief at my departure. But there is no sound, just the creak of the porch and my own protracted sigh. I refuse to believe that someone can live in a community and not know who the other inhabitants are. Unless they are protecting him. Any of the New Dawners could have scrubbed out my painting.

I am almost ready to abandon my visit to Foxleyhall, convinced that the truth about White is to be found at the New Dawn house, but remind myself that unless I investigate every possibility, take every step on the path, I cannot possibly hope to reach my destination. The old notion of progress dies hard.

Foxleyhall community is a sprawl of buildings standing in acres of fertile land which, according to Noah, produces healthy yields of vegetables and soya.

A child sits in the porch of the main house, playing with stones; it throws one up in the air, then picks as many up from the ground as possible with its throwing hand before trying to catch the first stone again without dropping any. Jacks. A game I've forgotten. I stand at a distance and watch.

This is the first child I have seen for many years. I have no idea what age or sex it is; it has long, wavy copper hair and round brown eyes that make my stomach lurch.

The child is getting further and further from success with each attempt. It looks up with an irritated glare, blaming me for its own inadequacies.

'Hello!' I call over.

The child drops its stones and scrambles to its feet. It bolts into the house, slamming the door behind it. I move a little closer to the house and wait, assuming the child has gone to fetch an adult. Eventually, when no one appears, I walk right up to the door. There is no knocker and my knuckles make little impact on the solid wood. I look over to the nearest window but curb the impulse to peer in. It is unlikely there is no one here; children are too precious to be left alone. I bang on the door once more with my forearm, more out of frustration than with any expectation of a response, then give up and leave.

When I arrive home someone has left a note at the mill door, held in place by a stone.

raychl i no sumthin that mite help cum 2 markit noah

I glance up and around in case he has waited for me to return, but there is no sign of anyone. Perhaps he has found out I am making investigations at the communities and wants to throw me off the scent before I visit his. Whatever it is, if I leave straight away I should catch him before he closes up for the night.

I am exhausted, my ankle is throbbing, but I head off down the lane.

He appears to be waiting for me, standing in the doorway of the market when I arrive, all smiles.

'Did you get my note?'

I nod as he watches me limp towards him.

'Come on in.'

I follow him to the back of the market and flop into the armchair.

'Are you limping?' he says.

'I tripped over on the stairs at home. It's fine now.'

'I've got stuff to put on it if you like.'

'No, it's okay, thanks. I've got stuff at home. What did you want to tell me?'

'Well, it isn't much; just something I remembered that happened a couple of years ago. Remember I said there are men at the New Dawn place?'

I nod.

'And what they do there?'

I nod again, but faster this time, trying to hurry him up. For a small thing he's making a meal of it.

'Well, a while ago, I heard that one of the men ran away. Escaped. Had his own romantic ideas about love and children and all that apparently, very old-fashioned, that didn't really fit with Momma's way of things. He'd fallen in love with one of the women and had to leg it before Momma could punish him. No one's ever seen him again, and not for the want of trying, I would imagine.'

'And?'

'That's it. You see, I was trying to work out how there can be someone living round here without me knowing them. It could only be someone from the New Dawn or someone who deliberately didn't want to be seen. Then I put the two together. If he's escaped from there he'd obviously need to keep his head down. Anyone who gets involved there is sworn to secrecy, and if they thought he was still around, giving away all their secrets, who knows what they might do to him.'

I'm struggling to imagine Momma raising her voice, let alone tracking someone down just because they don't want to live in her house, but the story fits with my gut reaction to today's visit. 'So, how do you know all this, if they're sworn to secrecy?'

Noah clears his throat. 'Ah, well, I became quite good friends with one of the women there and, er, she told me a few things she probably shouldn't have.'

I make a show of frowning, enjoying his embarrassment, but nonetheless feel a twinge of jealousy.

'But still, it all seems a bit far-fetched. Surely he would have left the area altogether?'

'Not necessarily. Where would he go? If he knows this area really well he's probably better off staying where he knows he can get food and water. Probably went back to where he lived before he went to the New Dawn.'

'Yes, you're right. It's probably him.'

'Great. Mystery solved, then?'

I switch from a frown to a smile.

'It looks like it, doesn't it?'

Noah looks very pleased with himself. A regular sleuth. 'Got time for some tea?'

'No, I won't, thanks. I need to get home. Thanks again.'

I haul myself out of the bottomless chair. Noah trails behind me to the door.

'I was looking for the red cat,' he says, as if I had asked. 'Have you seen him?'

'The squinty one? I saw it the time before last, in a doorway up there.' I point.

Noah shakes his head. 'That's where he always sits. He's disappeared since then. Ah well. See you soon.' He waves me on my way then goes back inside.

Someone is watching me. Watching me sleep. My eyes open and shift to one side. No other movement is possible; my body is frozen. I seem to have died in my sleep. A silver blur glimmers in the darkness. The watcher. The watcher smiles. I send her a conspiratorial smile in return. She quivers as if about to speak, then disappears, engulfed by a mist made of her own disappearing.

With no sleep left in me, I lie brooding upon the purpose of my psychic messenger. Is her message one of reassurance or of warning? I pick up the torch and flash it into each corner in turn; perhaps the intruder is to be found crouching in one of them. I up-end the torch on the floor and it casts my shadow long across the ceiling. I lever myself up into a sitting position and see the rest of the night out by amending my lists. Anything to bring the coming day closer.

17.9.43

When you find a girl, don't tell her you love her, show her. Protect her, watch over her. We are both artists, have both been betrayed. We should be together. We will be together. She cannot be contained or deceived, but once she is here I know she will choose to never leave. It has been decided by fate. I have been sent a sign. All lines of communication are down and my search is over. She is the one. I must prepare for her arrival for she will soon come.

white sheets x 2
white pillowcases with pink trim x 2
yellow blanket
blue blanket
pink flowery quilt

11.32am. full orgasm. missionary.

My next outing takes me to Noah's community, out on Weaste Lane. I am there at daybreak, watching through a gap in a rusted beech hedgerow. Noah leaves for the market on his bicycle. Another man, carrying a spade and a fork, heads out into the fields. Then two women, carrying a large basket between them, take off in the same direction. How happy they sound as the peaks of their chatter are thrown behind them on the breeze. A dark, curly head pops up from the basket. Another child. It has never occurred to me that there would be children in these communities. It must be considered safe to breed again now. Now that all my maternal longings have been quashed.

The little band disappears over the brow. I rise from my hiding place, legs stiff, pockets baggy with mushrooms picked to alleviate the boredom of watching, and sneak down the bank towards the house. My curiosity about this house extends well beyond the desire for information about White; this is Noah's home. Of the four communities it is the newest. Post-Jason.

With a hand to either side of my face to block out the light, I press my nose to the window. The room seems empty, but then a congeries of bright pictures, stuck higgledy-piggledy to the walls, comes into focus as my eyes adjust. A mess of children's toys is strewn across the floor: animal shapes carved from wood, large wooden cubes, triangles and spheres. A rocking horse. A vast rug made of sewn-together coats has been thrown down to protect tiny knees from nasty splinters.

Behind the house stands a tall windowless barn, fronted by a pair of wooden doors that run the full height of the building, the perfect hiding place for White's car. The doors are open and the rasp of a saw issues from within. I rush through the long grass towards the sound and press my body against the side wall of the barn. As I attempt to synchronise my breath with the rhythm of the saw, I contemplate my best course of action. Action, my new friend and ally.

Then the sawing stops. I hold my breath and the pounding of my heart fills the silence. I edge my way along the wall towards the doors. If he comes out now I will have a great view of him. If he sees me, I have a story rehearsed. And if it is White, I have a few questions that need answers.

I dare not move. I register the sound of shuffling feet and of someone whistling softly through their teeth. Then, being of the mind that it is better to discover than to be discovered, I step away from the wall and stroll into the gap between the open doors, squinting into the gloom. A large workbench stands at the back of the room, positioned so as to benefit from two large skylights above. No car. A man is inspecting the finish of a piece of planed wood. It is clear from his tall and wiry stature that this is not White. He holds the wood close to his face, running his fingers tenderly along its grain. I am invisible to him. If I were to turn and run now I could escape without being seen, but I am attracted by the warm smell of wood shavings, by the man with his long sensitive fingers, and the room with its odd wooden shapes decorating the walls, and I stay a beat too long. The man looks up.

He walks towards me, eyebrows raised in curious welcome. I like the way he looks; everything about him is pale as if faded with age. His pallor, it turns out, is due to a fine coating of sawdust that sticks to his hair and skin, lending him the appearance of finely sanded beech. His hair stands up in dark ash tufts, his eyes, chameleon eyes, the kind of eyes that adopt the colour of whatever it is they are looking at, are for now misty grey. He smiles, wipes a dry palm against his trouser leg and extends it towards me. Another forgotten ritual. I touch his rough-smooth hand with my own, and quickly let it go again.

'My dog has gone missing. I wonder if he has been by here?' I say. Why not? It sounded good in my head, and it still sounds all right now it's out there. The man frowns his concern.

'I don't think so. We've lost a couple of animals ourselves of late. People take them and eat them. What does he look like?' His voice is as dry as his appearance. Just listening to him makes me want to cough. I want to grab his hand and scrape the dust from under his fingernails.

'Black,' I say, 'with white markings.' I am thinking of the Home Farm dog, hoping he doesn't know him. 'He's a working dog but he's very friendly.'

'A sheepdog?'

I forget the names of things. I stare into the middle distance, lost for a moment in the depths of my own imagination. Then I stir myself, realising he is waiting for me to speak.

'What are you making?'

'I'll show you,' he says. He leads me over to the workbench and waves a hand over the various rounds and oblongs organised over its surface. 'I'm making a cart for the children.'

I mask my interest in his use of the plural by feigning puzzlement over an object hanging on the wall. 'What's that?'

'It's a violin, a fiddle, whatever you like to call it.'

'What's it for?'

'It's a musical instrument. For playing tunes.'

I am honestly impressed, both by his workmanship and by his patience in dealing with my pretended ignorance, but I cannot afford to let it undermine my performance; I keep up the charade.

'Can you play it for me?'

'Well, no, not without strings. It's not finished yet.' He moves closer to the wall and points at the violin. 'They will stretch from here to here. You make them sing by scraping across them with a bow. The body of the fiddle is hollow to amplify the sound.'

'Is this for the children too?'

'Ah, no. The eldest has one already; the youngest isn't ready yet.'

So only two. The child in the basket must be the youngest. Where is the eldest? I wonder if either of them is Noah's. My mind is full of questions, but I must curb my interest; I am supposed to be looking for a dog.

'We all play instruments here. We have great fun during the storms competing with the weather to see who can make the most noise. Where do you live?'

I have stayed too long; he isn't supposed to be asking me questions.

107

'Not far.' I make a vague gesture with my hand, in no particular direction.

'Then you must know Noah, down at the market?'

I purse my lips, as if trying to match the name to a face. He doesn't wait for my answer.

'Well, he plays a great guitar.'

I am on sticky ground here. If Noah finds out I have been sniffing around, especially now he thinks everything is resolved, he will be suspicious.

'Oh, it's my man always goes to the market.'

Already I have adopted his way of talking. That's what happens when you have no conversation in your life.

'What's your man's name?'

'Jez. Jez White. Do you know him?'

The dry man searches the sky for an appropriate memory. Then his head wobbles from side to side and he sticks out his bottom lip, which is strikingly red against his white skin. Nothing has come to light.

'And what's your name?'

'Daisy.' My grandmother's name, plucked out of memory, ha ha. Innocent. Fragile. Daisy White. I hold out my hand and smile. It's easy to be well mannered with this man.

'Now I must get going. It's been nice talking to you.'

Pleased with myself, but jumpy that someone else might show up, I twist my feet in the dust and turn to go.

'I'm Shady, by the way.' His voice pulls me back. 'What's his name?'

Momentarily confused, I stop and look back.

'The dog?' the man prompts.

Of course.

'Oh, he hasn't got one. We just call him dog.'

I am worried that someone might be drawn over, attracted by the voices. Once out of sight I attempt a semblance of a run, and scramble up the wooded slope to my original hiding place to work out my next move. My elevated position allows me a view over the hedge to the lane and I turn my head in that direction at the approach of a rhythmic creaking, like a magpie attempting to sing. Suddenly White appears round the bend, cycling fast, swerving and dodging, faster and faster, with the wind at his back. It is no wonder he has never been seen if he always travels at such speed. I duck behind a tree but he hasn't spotted me; his eyes are fixed on the road ahead. Then he's gone.

I half slide, half run towards the lane. There is no way I could catch him up. I set off in the opposite direction with the wind pushing against my chest like two giant hands. The physical effort slows my thoughts and the thrill of having seen him wanes from a boil to a simmer. At least I am sure now that I haven't invented him for my own entertainment. He was heading towards Warrington. I will search in that direction next. Clutching at straws, Jason would have said, but so what? I have a plan and I am hungry. They will feed me at the House of the New Dawn.

I am sitting in what has become my usual chair, with a plateful of crumbs on the table in front of me, and the fire blazing behind me. Momma is ladling tea into two bowls. The smell of molten wax drifts in from another part of the house. I am still hungry but dare not ask for more. I wonder when, or if, there is ever an occasion when all the places at this table are occupied.

Momma lowers herself into the seat opposite me.

'So what made you decide you would like to live here?' She says. 'Is id the food?' She smiles and I relax. Momma made a joke.

'I've been thinking about it for a while,' I say. I pause to emphasise what will come next, to make sure she is listening. 'There are things you don't know when you spend your life alone, like that when there's a storm coming in, the electricity in the air makes your hair stand on end. And a friend of mine has told me a little about what goes on here and I think it's something I would like to be a part of.'

Momma remains absolutely still, her smile relaxed and warm.

'Really? Which friend?'

'Jez.'

For a fleeting moment Momma is caught off guard. The fingers of her right hand lift involuntarily from the table, then gently lower, one by one, but her eyes stay on my face.

'Jason?' she says.

Now I am puzzled.

'No. Jez. Jez White. He used to live here.'

'Oh, yes, Jez.' She seems relieved. 'How is he? Is he still living nearby?'

'He's fine, thanks. Yes, fairly near.'

'Oh, yes.'

I struggle to read Momma's reaction. Will she send out a search party as soon as I have left, or is she making a mental note to have him killed? The thought that she might find him first bothers me.

'Did Jez tell you that he was breaking a rule of strict confidence giving you information aboud the New Dawn?'

'Oh, yes. I don't think he would have said anything if I hadn't said I was going to ask to move in.' It seems strange, defending White.

'Well Rachel, id may be possible for you to come here, but I must warn you that life here is very different from that to which you are accustomed. Why don'd you go away now and think aboud id some more? Then if you are still interested come back in a couple of days. I'll show you round and we can begin preparations for your integration.' Momma rises and picks up my plate. My *integration*.

I stand.

'Thank you, I'll do that. May I ask you one more question?'

'Of course.'

'Did Jason know what you do here?'

Momma puts the plate back on the table.

'Rachel, I suppose id is bedder that you know this. I am still in contact with Jason. He is nod very far away. You should know this if you are thinking of coming here, because his name is spoken here often.'

'Oh,' is all I can say. 'Yes.'

Momma walks to the door and opens it. 'I'll see you out.'

19.9.43

I'm taking too many risks. Today I was seen by that friend of his. After using my concealment so well, working hard to prepare something special for her arrival, I nearly blew it. But I suppose I'm over-excited. Now her friends are here and we're all waiting. Her room is ready. I couldn't wait any longer. I had to see where she is. Her place is a fortress, protected by walls and water, and no sign of her all day. Where is she? What if she is ill and in need of help? I'll wait one more day and then go in.

The key to Jason's study is in a drawer in the kitchen, exactly as he left it. I haven't so much as looked at it. Until now. It gleams up at me, shiny as temptation itself. The time has come to disturb the sanctity of Jason's den. I have turned the living room upside down, rifled through neglected art materials and other rubbish with a fine-tooth comb, as he would have insisted on had he been here, but all the time knowing I would not find what I was looking for and in the end would return to the key. Even so, with his imagined permission, I am not quite brave enough to touch the key without pulling my sleeve down over my fingers to avoid contaminating the precious metal. Old habits die hard.

The lock's barrel turns easily and the door swishes inwards, fanning the halitosis smell of a room that has been denied light and air for many seasons. I switch on the overhead light and remove the key from the lock before stepping into the room. Just in case.

The desk and bookcase are shrouded in bedsheets that have yellowed with age. The boxes I want are easy to find.

I fold back a corner of the sheet between thumb and middle finger to reveal a low bookcase where Jason's map collection is arranged in neat sequential order. Each box is clearly labelled in his handwriting.

I pull out *Maps – Local*, working it free from its neighbours, and place it on the desk. A cloud of dust puffs into the stagnant air and tickles the hairs of my nose. I sneeze it back out and two little pearls of snot settle on the lid, which I wipe clean with a corner of the sheet. I lift the lid, revealing a compacted row of pink spines, and ease out the map marked *Warrington, Lymm & Surrounding Areas.* I replace the lid and return the box to its proper place.

Clutching the map to my chest, I check the room for any incriminating signs of disturbance, lock the door behind me and return the key, careful to place it precisely inside the invisible outline of its original position.

The map has aged despite its lack of use. I spread it out on the table, respectful of its crumbling seams; it must be at least thirty years old. Many of the areas it shows to be above sea level have long since been waterlogged, swamped by sea, river, or an overwhelmed drainage system. Using the mill as my starting point, I trace an outward spiral, a possible search route. My fingers smear a light dust-trail over the terrain, an unintended but realistic parody of the permanent cloud cover that dogs me.

The areas north of the Bridgewater Canal and west of the Ship Canal are uninhabitable flood plain and so provide a natural border. The motorway-turned-vehicle-dump, a long, silent, rusting traffic jam, which extends far to the south, and the Chester road to the east, square the zone off nicely. I mark the boundaries of my hunting ground in pencil so they can be easily erased should Jason return. Each building is represented by a little box, of which there are hundreds, if not thousands, some scattered, others in clusters, and any one of them is potentially White's home. I refold the map, pushing it at each end like a pair of bellows, and hide it away in a kitchen cupboard. I prepare the house for the night and brace myself for the encroaching northerly gale.

In the morning, I spread the map one last time before setting out. My ankle is more painful than ever but there is no time to lose. Poring over the map's multitude of squares and squiggles, I attempt to commit them all to memory, and with the new day the scale of my task begins to dawn. I stash the map in its hiding place, then stand at the stove and deliver a few absent-minded spoonfuls of cold soup to my mouth before I leave. Ah, procrastination, I remember you well.

Dunham village is a mess of broken glass, collapsed roofs and burned-out cars. Most of the smaller buildings are inaccessible, some even invisible, thanks to the jungle of trees and shrubs that have fallen or thrived in the absence of care. The wooden planks that protected the pub windows now dangle from their fixings or lie rain-warped on the ground.

Further on, a cluster of canal-side houses is guarded by a row of mature conifers, one of which has forced its topmost branches through an upstairs window. The frames of the other windows have been emptied, unbroken glass being a precious commodity nowadays. Their paintwork has split and peeled like skin chafed by the incessant wind. I enter the nearest house.

The downstairs room is bisected horizontally by a filthy brown tidemark, stinks of algae and damp and is stripped bare of all decoration and colour but for a small red wooden cube that sits on the mouldy carpet. A child's brick, which probably escaped notice by being hidden under a chair or sofa. I swing at it with the handle of the umbrella; it ricochets off the wall and lands close to the light brown square that marks its original position. I pick it up and put it in my pocket. There is no life here. I am wasting time.

On the towpath, heavy raindrops part the tiny leaves of the canal's algae carpet. A moorhen dashes across it, heading for cover. For me the going is treacherous, but the spike of my umbrella prods finger-shaped wells into the mud and keeps me on my feet.

By the time the mill comes into view I am exhausted and my ankle is throbbing. First the roof of my house, and then my bedroom window, peep over the top of the storm wall. I imagine myself there, a pale face behind the distant glass, an imprisoned princess, looking out at an unfamiliar figure on the canal path. Whoever it was I saw out here must have been standing in the exact spot that I now occupy.

Although the mill is within spitting distance, Jason destroyed the footbridge for extra protection, so I have to walk home the long way. The steps down into Little Bollington are so overgrown they may as well not be there. All the buildings on this side of the river are visible from my bedroom window; I already know none of them has been lived in for years. A whole day wasted. At this rate I will never find him. Preparation is everything, Jason would have said.

My boot is tight where my ankle has swelled again and my hips ache from the pressure of constantly shifting my weight onto my good side, my shoulder from leaning on the umbrella.

I arrive home shivering, wet and deflated. I wrap myself in blankets and settle down to study the map again, in the vain hope that perhaps a vital clue has planted itself there while I was out, preferably in the form of a big X or an arrow, at the same time aware how disappointed I would be to have it all spelled out for me; how frustrating it would be to be denied the challenge that is coaxing me back to a life beyond mere survival, and reintroducing the idea of possibility, if not of hope, to my claustrophobic existence.

I draw crosses through all the buildings checked in today's outing. It doesn't amount to much and most of them could have been crossed off without leaving the house. I write the day off as a learning exercise, but two things occur to me. Any sign of life would be more easily detected at night; a speck of candlelight, a moving shadow, a smoking chimney, would all be more visible in darkness. And I could travel, and escape if necessary, much more quickly if I didn't have to walk. The wagon would be too conspicuous even if I could restore it, but Jason's bicycle is still in the garage.

Satisfied that something positive has come of the day's fruitless outing, I pick up my *Woyzeck* and lie down to read. But for the first time ever it bores me, and I am unable to stay awake beyond the first few words.

I am ready to leave at dusk. Jason's bike is rusty but the chain seems to be working all right. I have plundered his head torch and stretched it round my hard hat so that if I am seen my face will at least be in the shadow of its downward beam. All essentials for the outing have been listed and crammed into my rucksack. I check the list one last time: *map (✔), pencil (✔), bread (✔), water bottle (✔), puncture kit (✔), torch (✔), list (✔).*

I soon discover that travelling by bicycle is no easier than walking; the tyres are almost flat and I didn't think to look for the pump. The head torch casts too high a beam to be of much benefit and my neck aches from having to dip my head while simultaneously raising my eyes to see where I am going.

At the top of Agden Brow I stop to catch my breath. I switch off my torch and blindness closes in. I switch it on again. A dead tree springing to life above the hedge gives me a fright.

On the outskirts of Lymm I come off the main road into an estate, its houses set in neat rows and in varying stages of dereliction. Once, they were all identical, distinguishable only by the differences in their owners' gardening skills or taste in window dressings. Now their façades are masked by creepers that poke and delve into business that is no longer anyone's but their own.

A huddle of houses arranged in a circle around a central green feign a community interest that never existed when people lived here. The green's heart is host to the charred remains of a car bonfire, entangled in brambles, but there is no sign of recent human activity so I move on, wheel spokes ticking in the night air.

The long route up Booth's Hill is my only option since the bridge over the reservoir, still intact if you believed the map, was blown up by Jason and his cronies. I pull the torch down to relieve my stiffening neck and its beam plays about the front wheel, producing a flickering strobe effect. It is raining; dark specks of shadow appear on the torch's reflected light before I feel anything. At the top of the hill I get lost in the maze of unremarkable streets and have to guess when I have covered them all.

I am home well before dawn. After a bowl of lukewarm soup I spread the map again and cross out all ground covered so far. I draw a circle round Noah's community. There are only two areas White could have been heading for when he passed Noah's place that I have not already searched. I select one of them, Grappenhall, as my next destination, circle it and draw an arrow along Weaste Lane connecting it to the circle round Noah's place. Not strictly necessary, but it looks great; like the spectacles I drew as a child on all the photographs of my father, but with one lens broken. Rational thought succumbs to animal instinct. I am on his trail.

I stretch out my aching limbs and consider the soporific possibilities of mentally constructing the next day's timetable, but before I have even begun, I am asleep.

I wake with something bothering me, a single thought that has been rising in me like sap since my visit to the communities. Some of the children there are old enough to have been born when Jason and I were still together. He lied to me about the safety of breeding. Tricked me out of motherhood, the one thing that would have made me strong. Jason knew about the babies at the House of the New Dawn and must have known about those at the other places.

I get up and distract myself from a reaction I am not ready for by lowering the shutters in all the rooms. I decide to keep them closed from now on, day and night, regardless of the weather. My home is my bunker, my wartime command centre.

The remains of the lentil soup are too pungent to eat, even for me. I prepare a fresh pot using nettles and the last of the vegetables and set it to simmer on the stove while I calm myself by perusing the positive. I have at least rediscovered the direct link between eating and living. It's a start. To exist without physical nourishment is to function at the most basic level, a level at which little may be achieved. I dampen a chunk of bread and throw it in the oven to warm through then settle down on the sofa, not sleeping, not thinking. Resting. I tell myself the churning in my belly is hunger, rather than anger at Jason and grief for my wasted past. I cannot rest.

I get up again and prepare for my next trip; I pump up the tyres on the bike, gouge dried mud and grit from their tread. The horizon is clear and the wind has slowed to a light but chill northwesterly. I pack an extra sweater, just in case, and set off with the bitter tang of nettles on my tongue. The hunt is on.

By the time I reach Noah's community, it is pitch dark. I dismount and push the bike, keeping close to the hedgerow to avoid being seen from the house. The swish of the tyres on the wet road is amplified in the night's stillness, but I imagine the noise level inside the house would easily cover it: children squealing, adults chatting, perhaps even the reedy mingling of voices and scratchy violin. Having a singsong. Smoke curls above the chimneystack. I stop for a moment to peer through the hedge. Their shutters are still open, but there is nothing to see except the occasional flicker of human activity.

I push on to a safe distance then remount, not switching my lamp on until certain of being out of sight. I am perfecting the art of stealth.

The map shows a tight row of houses to one side of the lane beyond Noah's house. There are six in all, divided into two lots of three by a ginnel. I doubt that White lives here, he would be too exposed. I carry on down the road. Further on it disappears under the canal by means of a tunnel of indeterminate length in the darkness. My front wheel hits what I think is a puddle. I thrust one foot to the ground to stop the bike and plunge knee-deep into cold black water. The tunnel is flooded. The enormous value of swearing is only truly realised on occasions such as these. Shit, fuck, bastard. I scoot myself backwards onto dry ground and stand, elbows on handlebars, glaring into the tunnel while I decide what to do next. The sound of a stone tossed into a puddle or pond can give some indication of the water's depth; I hold the bike steady with one hand while I scrabble on the ground with the other. A bright splash is what I am hoping for, but an intimidating plop is what I get. So deep it has no echo. There is no choice but to continue, so, with my skirts pulled up and tied at the hip and my trousers rolled up over my knees, I brace myself and push the bike at full arm stretch into the dead water, the front wheel searching for underwater obstructions. A freezing droplet nips at the back of my craning neck.

No one in their right mind would make this their regular route to anywhere. But then, no one in their right mind would pretend to be someone else. The road slopes upwards again and I drag my stinging feet out to the lane on the other side.

I sit down on the ground to remove my boots and socks and revive my feet in the relative warmth of my skirts. I wring the water from my socks and tie them to the handlebars to dry. Not that they will. I use my skirts to mop the insides of my boots before tying them back onto my bare feet.

Hundreds of flashing eyes follow me as I wheel my bike past row after row of small terraced cottages, occupied only by extended families of cats, who watch with interest as I progress over scatterings of broken glass and the soft cushions of grass that punctuate the road's surface. How permanent this all seemed before, and how flimsy now. How quickly the materials of an age decompose.

Where nothing lives is surely death. As a rule, the proximity of other living, breathing humans only heightens my sense of isolation, whereas an encounter with their ghosts and mediators brings solace. There is strange comfort in the company of hidden creatures and forgotten lives. There is life here. Life in abundance. Just not human life. For cats to survive in such numbers there must be mice, rats, birds. At night this place is seething with vitality; and by day life's representatives are the ivy and creepers that can simultaneously hold up and pull down whole buildings. I am conspicuous here. Mentally cast adrift from my mission, I am behaving more like someone hoping to be found, to be the conquered and not the conqueror. Does it really matter which? Enough; he is not here.

The rough inners of my boots rub at the soft parts of my feet, drawing out raw points that will develop into blisters. He is not here. I know it; the cats know it. I lost the scent at the tunnel. We are playing hide and seek and I can sense whether I am warm or not. Not only am I not warm, I am a disconnected satellite, cut off from any link to him.

In my distraction I almost miss the aberration in the hedgerow to my left. Someone has built a dry-stone wall across the entrance to a lane. I rest my bike on the ground and investigate. The top of the wall is about level with my forehead; to see over it I have to poke my toe around to find a gap large enough to accommodate my boot, then, placing my hands on top of the wall, heave myself up. I balance there, one leg dangling, squinting into the pitch black beyond. I am onto something, warm again. My free leg scrambles for another hold, I push up further, and before I know it I have dropped to the other side, landed on my weak ankle, and brought one of the top stones down behind me. My skirts are trapped under me and they rip as I struggle to my feet. I pull the trailing material away and throw it to one side.

The going is more difficult without a torch, but safer, I think. To deaden my footsteps I follow the soft grassy seam that marks the centre of the lane. Overhead a lark bursts into song, and sure enough the sky above the canal bank is brightening. A vampire's panic rises in me and common sense nags at me to turn back. But common sense has yet to win its first battle where I am concerned.

I'm right to keep going because into the near distance looms the silhouette of a rooftop. Attached to the roof is a chimney, and above the chimney a trail of white smoke is engaged in a cycle of evaporation and renewal. Fire. Life. Fires don't light themselves. Not in this weather.

The house sits within a grassy rectangle, which has been shorn into a neat square carpet. I move closer in to the shadow of the hedge, edging forward for a clear view of the front porch beside which sits a paunchy water butt. Four evenly spaced oblong windows watch over the lane. A smaller, round window sits like a spy-hole between the upstairs two. With the exception of the round one, shutters cover all the windows. Whoever lives here has not yet risen.

The lane continues beyond the house, and a little way further on are two smaller buildings. Keeping to the grass to muffle my footsteps, I hurry past the side of the house. There are four oblong patches of lighter brick in the back wall where the north-facing windows have been bricked up for protection against the evil north winds.

The first of the two outbuildings is a scaled-down version of Shady's barn, with double doors that open directly onto the lane. The second is a cottage, its windows intact but unprotected, its miniature front garden a tangle of brambles. Rampant hedgerow and more brambles have engulfed it from behind. Beyond the cottage the lane bends towards the canal then disappears. Standing here in the early dawn, sheltered from the wind and serenaded by a rising crescendo of birdsong, it is hard to stay alert to potential danger, no matter who lives here. Someone lives here. I am trespassing.

I try the door to the cottage and find it unlocked. It opens directly onto a staircase, with open doorways to either side. I go in and close the door softly behind me. The first room is unfurnished but for an old-fashioned telephone, still connected to a socket in the wall. The floor is carpeted twice; once with a rough woollen matting, and covering that a thick layer of dust. The other room is a kitchen. Or rather it was. All that remains is a stove, and one cupboard, fixed to the wall at waist height. The cupboard is empty but for a single brass key on its bottom shelf.

This room is twice the length of the other and yet from the outside the cottage is a complete square. At the darkest end of the kitchen I discover a door in the side wall. It is locked, but a messy quarter-circle is etched into the lino by its frequent opening and closing. I take the key from the cupboard and try it in the lock. The door scrapes open to reveal nothing but blackness so dense that the feeble light from the room behind me stands no chance of penetrating. I curse my lack of a torch. The air inside is dank and chill, tinged with an unidentifiable rotting smell; probably it has been used for storage, maybe for fruit and vegetables, or as a workshop. I lock the door and replace the key.

The two upstairs rooms are unremarkable and empty. I am about to run a finger through the dust on the windowsill of one when I hear a sharp bang from the direction of the house. Outside my line of vision, someone is crossing from the house towards the cottage, their feet crunching on the loose stones. Even with my head squeezed so far into the corner that it hurts, I cannot see who it is. They have stopped at the barn. I daren't open the window to look out. The rasp of a bolt being drawn back; a door sliding open and then shut again; the bolt slamming home. Then I see him. It is White. Pushing his bike. He stops beneath my window, so close that I could spit directly onto the thinning crown of his head, onto the neat bull's-eye of pink flesh that shows through the yellow hair. I sense his clean baby smell and it turns my stomach.

The rucksack on his back is flaccid. He places his left foot on one pedal and swings his other leg over the crossbar in a movement of such contrived elegance that I wonder if he knows I am watching. He coasts away towards the canal, the ratchet creak of his pedal speeding up as he goes, to where there must be another way out onto Weaste Lane.

I crawl through the dust to the next room, but he is already out of sight. I should leave now, take the opportunity to escape, but this may be my only chance to find out about him. I go quietly down the stairs and open the front door to check the lane. For all I know there may be a woman here, children even. But instinct tells me there are not. Instinct tells me that White is like Jason, the kind of man who would stamp on a spark for fear of being outshone. I walk over to the house. The shutters are now open and I press my face to the nearest downstairs window.

The glass is cold against the tip of my nose. I could be looking back in time, into a room in my grandparents' house. Its walls and floor are of dark polished wood and two short sofas form an L-shape round the cold open fireplace. White's house is a home in waiting. Through the next window is a kitchen.

The front door is unlocked. I push it open and lean in, taking a moment to measure the air.

'Hello?' I wait. 'Hello-o.' No reply.

I remove my boots and hide them behind the water butt. I go in.

The door to the room I looked in at is closed. The kitchen door is open. A pair of long glass doors looks out onto a hedgerow and the raised bank of the canal beyond. Neat and spotless, White's home is a well-preserved monument to the distant past. But the smell of fried eggs lingers above the stove as a reminder of its present occupation. My hands hover above the hotplate to catch the rising heat.

I run up the stairs. There are two bedrooms, one in faded pink, its bed-for-two covered in rose floral quilting. The charms of the second bedroom are easier to resist; it is decorated in blue and black, and is stark and cold. Next to the bed is a clock, its ticking amplified by the table on which it stands. I lean in to inspect it without touching: a simple mechanism, with two knobs at the back, one for winding and another for moving the hands. I remember. Beside it is a torch, similar to my own, a telephone handset and a large yellow book and pencil, above them a bedside lamp.

The book's cover bears the invisible marks of regular use. If I stare at it long enough perhaps I can read its contents without touching it. I run a fingertip over its rough surface. No dust. With a casual flick I lift the cover.

It floats upwards, offers a teasing glimpse of scrawl, then falls back into place. I snatch the book up and dash with it across the landing to the pink room.

The only source of external light in both bedrooms is a small circular window in each side wall. The pink room overlooks the lane and has a good view of the garage and half of the cottage, although not of its front door. I open the book at the beginning.

The handwriting is almost illegible; I have to hold the book at arm's length and turn it into the light to make out the words, the internal ramblings of a lonely mind. White's mind. The first entry is old. I do the calculation; it is dated six years before the entry that follows it.

21.5.37
I must prepare myself.

She'll come. I've seen her in the far-off, approaching slow. Her heavy boots push up and down in the peaty slush, and tickle the tiny pink stars that cling to the rocks. Her thigh and calf muscles form a stripe from hip to knee, then knee to woollen sock as she marches and hums. She's still too distant for me to see the movement of her mouth, but the sound of her soft utterances floats through the ether like the Siren's lull. Her hair streams behind like oil, balances the forward movement of her sleek determined head.

Here in this room with me, next to me. Or maybe over there. Free-spirited, she'll choose the armchair, tuck her feet into the rear right-hand corner of the cushion, calf muscle flexed hard. The rolled cuff of

her sock embossing the back of her silken thigh,
where only I will see it. I'll trace its pocky texture
with my tongue.

These must be the old-fashioned romantic notions that Noah was talking about. Despite myself I find it quite endearing. I resume my flicking, through pages and pages of lists, of clothes worn and washed and worn again, interspersed with yearning for someone called Paloma; everything is dated and timed to the nearest second. Then something catches my eye. I stop and turn back a few pages.

11.42am	*fox*	*headless*	*taken*
12.10pm	*bird*	*broken wing*	*left*
12.32pm	*squirrel*	*teeth*	
14.22pm	*chicken*	*fresh*	*taken*

White is an animal-lover. Maybe even an animal-saviour, which renders him harmless, if not something of a hero. All the same, I cannot risk him finding me here. A love of animals is an attractive quality but explains nothing.

I return the book to the blue room and hurry downstairs and out of the house. The door thuds shut behind me. I slip my feet into my boots, hitch up my skirts and run back up the lane, then scramble over the wall to safety.

My bike and bag are as I left them, my socks still sopping wet. I rummage in my bag for a mouthful of something to still my nerves. As I sink my teeth into the stale bread I use my free hand to unfold the map. Now I know where it is, White's lane is easy to locate. There are the house, the barn and the cottage, all reduced to innocent oblongs. The other end of his lane goes under the canal and comes out somewhere behind the six houses on Weaste Lane.

I work out a long route home that will lessen the chances of running into either Noah or White, but unfortunately I cannot avoid the flooded tunnel. I repack my bag, and brace myself for another soaking.

As I lie on the sofa at home I imagine myself in that house, in the pink bedroom, the soup bubbling on the stove downstairs, waiting for White to return. Why not him? It's true I don't find him physically attractive, but I've been comparing him to Noah, and Jason. Perhaps I've misjudged him. Sometimes romantic, sensitive people do things that might seem extreme or even insane to others. Does it matter how you meet someone? It's quite clear that Noah doesn't want me. When it all boils down, if what we want is to be with another person, does it really matter who it is?

I sleep all day and wake as daylight fades. It would seem that as I slept some decisions have been made.

Under cover of darkness I collect four eggs and make a potato omelette to take with me, adding to it the shrivelled mushrooms that I picked in the woods outside Noah's house.

When my bag is stuffed with everything I need – water, bread, omelette, torch, spare socks, map, blanket – I set off with it digging uncomfortably into the knobbles of my spine.

My thigh muscles strain with the effort of pedalling into the wind. The strap of my hard hat rubs a red patch under my chin as its rim pushes back off my forehead. I duck my head and cycle blind.

The scene at Noah's house is the same as the night before; nonetheless I follow my precautionary routine: stop, torch off, and push the bike safely past. The sweat dries on my back, but I continue to walk in darkness until I reach the row of houses that shields the exit from White's lane. Once there, I switch on the torch, swing its beam into the ginnel and push my bike through onto a cobbled lane. I turn in the direction of White's house. To my left a high wall hides the back yards of the houses, while the other side is lined by a ditch, out of which a steep bank climbs up to the canal. It is peaceful here, sheltered from the wind;

all is quiet but for the tick of my bike chain and the whirr of a bat's wings.

I suck in the night air; take my first conscious breath since leaving the road. The lane bends round to the right and disappears under the canal. I flash the torch onto the tunnel floor. Its beam bounces off shining cobbles, which are wet but thankfully not flooded. I hide my bike behind a clump of hawthorn near the tunnel's entrance.

The cobbles slope upwards, and thanks to the incessant dripping from above are slippery underfoot. The wall is too slimy to offer much in the way of support and I have forgotten to bring my umbrella. But soon my feet grip at a rougher surface and the tunnel wall gives way to a chain-link fence.

My hand reaches out for the wire but grabs instead at something soft and spongy. I drop the torch and it clatters onto the cobbles and rolls away. I scrabble around in the dark until I find it, switch it on and train its beam to my left. The fence is an expanse of diamond-shaped holes, each one stuffed with the body of a dead bird. Starlings. Hundreds of them. Driven into the fence by a storm and unable to dislodge themselves.

I lower the beam towards the ground as a mark of respect and resume my steady shuffle towards White's house. The cottage roof comes into view first, a black triangle against an enormous bruise of a sky.

Shadows appear and dissolve in the darkness. I become one of them and dart for the back wall of his house; my feet make a ripping sound on the loose stones. I stick my head out and round the side wall and focus my attention on the hedge opposite, scan it for any glimmer of reflected light, but see none so I reckon the shutters are closed. I turn back towards the cottage; it's hard to believe that it was just this morning I was here. But it becomes all too easy when I open the cottage door and the torchlight picks out the imprint of my heavy boots in the dusty stair carpet. It is one thing to have come looking for him, but it is a different matter if he knows I've found him before I am ready to offer myself up.

In my horror I allow the door to shut rather too sharply behind me. Swearing under my breath, I switch off the torch, edge into the front room and crouch down to wait for him to come rushing over to investigate. He doesn't. I give up and go upstairs.

I shine the torch into both upstairs rooms before installing myself in the same one as before. I already think of this room as mine. If we were together this would be a perfect little cottage for me to work in. I pick at chunks of omelette and wonder how long I should wait. I study the map until impatience gets the better of me. This is what it would be like, I tell myself, sitting around waiting for him to come back from wherever it is he goes every day. But there is something I can do to pass the time.

I go downstairs to the kitchen and take the key to the secret room from the cupboard. The torch beam encircles the lock and I slide the key home. What was an unpleasant smell this morning is a rotten stench tonight. I raise the beam. My heart leaps as an off-kilter stare flashes back at me.

How did you get in here? The words form themselves but before they can be whispered I detect an altered quality, a diminished intensity, in the red cat's stare. And the cat's body is not a cat's body but the body of a fox. The fox's tail is not the tail of a fox but the tail of a squirrel. The three sections of this monstrous creation are held together by giant crude stitches.

There is more: the head of the black and white dog, its tongue lolling out of its mouth, is too heavy for its body, the body of the off-kilter ginger. It has keeled over onto the bench and twisted the rigid body into a grotesque contortion, which in turn has knocked over a blue bucket, *my* blue bucket. Four stumps prod upward where its legs should be; a work in progress.

Gagging, I clamp my hand tight over my mouth and rush for the door. A few moments later, the stinking combination of half-digested nettle soup and potato omelette, warmed by my body, is splashing into the foliage behind the cottage.

Fuelled by an overwhelming need to escape, I force myself back into the cottage, and with shaking hands reseal the tomb and return the key. Then I run, with the devil at my back. Tears streak my face as I stumble through the tunnel to my bike and I am halfway home before it dawns on me. At a safe distance I stop to rinse my mouth of the taste of vomit only to realise I have left my drinking water, and my bag with it, in the cottage. But I can't go back now.

Home. Unable to sleep, tormented by the constant rhythm of the rain, my thoughts are stuck in a loop, spewing out from a common source like wool off a spindle and weaving together into the most terrible outcomes imaginable. I censor the revolving images of mutilated animals and of White's own naked, scrawny body, mutilated and sewn together by me, and recite instead the contents of my abandoned rucksack. From the little he already knows about me there is nothing in it that can be traced back to me, or identify me as someone he knows. Except the map.

Every circle, cross, and arrow on it links my world to his. It helped me to find him, and it could so easily reverse the favour and lead him straight to me. I'll have to go back.

I attempt to calm myself into sleep by rationalising the urgency of the situation. There is indeed a risk of his finding my bag, but not before tomorrow. And even then it could belong to anyone, a jobber maybe, or someone from the New Dawn come to get him.

It is still not dawn when I come to. I have hardly slept and my mind is full of the night's horrors. I get up and wash the metallic tang of vomit from my tongue.

My first instinct is to carry on with life as normal, to be active; there are vegetables rotting in the ground, nettles to pick, firewood to chop. I decide to go out now, before daylight, when I will be less easily spotted. I need to think. The trouble with thinking used to be that it would open the floodgates to the past, but now, by comparison to the present, the past seems a place of safety, dogged only by petty squabbles. Jason and me in our living room. Jason caressing the plans of the mill that show everything as it was then: the river split in two to negotiate the island; the weir, the mill, our house, all perfectly to scale and represented in the most minute detail. And, shaded in grey, everything as it would be, and is now: the wind turbine, the water filters, and the storm wall that runs the length of the lane and circles the island in the shape of a mutant tadpole, or a sperm, or a noose; it could be any of these, depending on his mood. All under control. Present and future precisely drawn. His solution to my nightmare vision of what was to come. His project, our separate salvations.

I am there in the background, fidgeting around behind him, pacing from one window to the next and back again, bleached by shafts of April sunlight. The windows are wide open and the scent of hogweed and elderflower mask the dank river smell, but not my agitation. On the river bank opposite, cows in mud socks pull at the long grass.

'Does it really need to be that high? It will block out all the light,' I am saying. 'I need light to paint by.'

His millionth explanation is delivered in a tone that, superficially at least, echoes the patience of his first.

'Only down here, and then not all of it. That's quite a wide corridor between the house and the wall.' He slides his finger in an arc over the plans. 'We'll paint it white, which will help. Anyway, when the weather gets really bad the shutters will be down and there'll be no light then in any case.'

I sniff. Even without looking at me he knows I am about to cry.

'I want to paint a mural. A progression. To show how things change,' I say.

'Yes, I know, but what's more important, our survival or a few pretty pictures?' His harshest words are always delivered in his most soothing voice. He smooths his hair away from his forehead in order to look at me more squarely.

I rub a fingertip against the windowpane knowing its squeaking will pick at his nerves, and feel him brace himself for my speech: the one about how I was beginning to wish I'd kept my ideas to myself, and perhaps it would be better to just take whatever life threw at us. There is no point in repeating it because he only ever half listens, he is too busy waiting for the opportunity to reel off the same tired answers: maybe this is it, maybe this is what life has thrown at you, at us, at everyone. He would win; we both know it, know that inwardly I crave the isolation the wall will provide. I stop the squeaking and thump towards the door.

'I'm going to lie down,' I say.

'Oh, great. I work my arse off getting this right. All for you, I might add. And all you can do is slink off to bed at eleven minutes past three in the afternoon. A-fucking-gain.'

There is nothing to be gained by him saying that again either, but it doesn't stop him.

Once upstairs I concentrate on radiating the force of my anger through the bedroom floor into the living room below, on projecting a weight of expectation – apology, conciliatory cups of tea, contrite smiles – down onto the crown of his head. I will him to climb the stairs and make the first move towards appeasement. The usual routine. Because we both know that no matter what happens he remains dependent on my approval.

But instead of coming upstairs he switches on the radio, turns it up loud so that single piano notes break the tension like the first stars on a midsummer's evening. Chopin. I imagine him watching the ceiling, waiting for my thumping objection from above; picture him folding the plans into a neat square and spreading his hands above them, closing his eyes and taking himself away, inside, to his very centre, where all is calm and good and right and true, and nothing exists but breath, life itself.

The phone rings and the music stops. I hear the warm lilt of his muffled words, his tone altered to the charming one he reserves for everyone but me. Then all is quiet. He has gone out without slamming the door.

I run into his study and watch him march off down the lane. As he stretches the distance between him and the mill, between us, his pace relaxes, soothed by the sunshine that coats the grass with silver and seduces the perfume from elderflower and campion. Later, he tells me about the whirlwind. To make me jealous.

He hears a rustling amongst the trees and turns his head towards the disturbance. A clutch of dead leaves bob weightlessly over the long grass, as if a frantic creature running in ever wider and more demented circles is kicking them up to be caught and held by gravity. They spread out into a broader funnel as if being stirred from above by an invisible giant finger. I wish I had the language to describe the intensity of his voice in the telling of this tale, its reverential wonderment, but such description is beyond me. Suffice it to say that it grates on my nerves.

He has never seen a whirlwind before. He stands mesmerised in its path, not daring to breathe for fear of disturbing its fragile formation. It passes over him, gathering him for a moment into its gentle vortex, then floats on towards a clearing, where it sways, unsure of its next move, then crumples and scatters over the roots of an up-ended oak. Gone. As if it had never been. He experiences a strange mixture of privilege and rejection. Wanker.

It was not long after this that work began on the wall, and Jason was too preoccupied to be overly concerned by my refusal to involve myself in the project. 'Are you sick?' he would ask at first, in a genuine attempt to entice me out of the bedroom or at least to leave the confines of the bed. I was happy for him to bring me meals upstairs and then leave me alone. Refusing his frequent offers to update me on progress outside was a form of entertainment for me. 'Don't you want to come and have a look?' he would say. 'The turbine will be up tomorrow.' Eventually he gave up.

A small black cat that sits watching me dig stirs me back to the present. His curious gaze bothers me. I want to shoo him away: shoo, devil cat. Since my discovery of White's 'sculptures' I am convinced that any kind of interaction with me will condemn the poor creature to a mutilated end. So I leave the potato patch and go in search of nettles and hope he won't follow.

By the same token I wonder if the child at Foxleyhall is in danger. Its own instincts told it to run away from me, but I can do nothing to protect it from White. Am I being punished by some cruel unforgiving god for deferring responsibility for my privileged vision to Jason, for dishing it out muse-like and willy-nilly to some lesser mortal? Is this the past catching up with me as Jason said it would, or is it my chance to correct the balance?

I hurry home with my wheelbarrow of vegetables: potatoes, carrots, onions, a huge wilting bundle of nettles, all rain-soaked and gleaming. I hustle the chickens into their houses, their welfare suddenly paramount. Was it White who stole my chicken? I hide the still-laden wheelbarrow in the workshop and set out on my bike just as dawn is breaking over the park.

I get it now. My challenge is to be the avenger of White's abominations against nature, and the defender of any he may have planned for the future. Only the lucky and the blessed get a second chance in life; this could be mine. But I may need a refuge, and there is only one place I can go where White can't come after me.

Momma is surprised to see me back again so soon and, as I was hoping, seems to take it as a sign of my determination and commitment. She brings me into the kitchen and offers me the standard fare, but I have no stomach for it. Momma manages to look simultaneously concerned and disapproving of my refusal and insists I dry myself by the fire before we begin our tour of the house. She drags my chair so close to the flames that when I sit down they draw steam from my clothes.

'Of course, I will nod be showing you the birthing rooms today, you understand,' she says, and I am confused. Her words are not intended to punish me for refusing food, or else I would change my mind and feign hunger. There is no edge to her voice. She must have a good reason. Perhaps someone is in labour and doesn't wish to be disturbed. Everyone has secrets from which I must be excluded.

The heat of the fire dries my throat, and when Momma offers a second time I am glad to accept a bowl of tea.

'How many people live here?' I say.

'We have sixteen adults altogether. Six mothers, four attendants, plus me, and Lara, who you med before.'

I make the calculation in my head. Presumably the other four are the men. Will I ever be told about them? And how many babies? Where *are* the babies? Where are their toys?

'I'm sure you have many questions, but I'm sure things will stard to become clear once we take a look around,' says Momma.

141

As soon as I have finished my tea Momma stands, but gestures at me to stay where I am.

'I will go see if everything is ready for us.'

Already I am disappointed. I was hoping to see the community in its normal everyday state, not a special, tidied-up version of it. Momma leaves the room. Someone must have been waiting all this time on the other side of the door, listening, for as soon as the door is closed the murmur of low voices starts up. Then Momma returns.

'Are you ready? Please pud these on your feed.'

She hands me a pair of hand-sewn slippers made of a soft flowery fabric. Stephanie would refuse point-blank, and even I can see they look ridiculous, but I accept that they must be worn as part of a necessary humiliation process.

'Be careful nod to slip on the tiles,' Momma says.

As I guessed, the slippers aren't even practical. We cross the hall and Momma opens a door into a room at the back of the house.

'This is the workshop. We make candles in here and other idems thad we can use and also trade ad the market.'

The room is empty of people but the smell of molten wax lingers. Light floods in through a pair of west-facing glass doors that open out onto a garden, and the room is warm with the heat of a massive stove that fills most of one wall. I could paint in this room.

Three large metal pans, used I presume for melting wax, stand on the stove and across the room a potter's wheel sits idle. Two long workbenches, strewn with various tools, are divided by a long metal bath over which a single tap drips into a metal bucket. Not at all tidy, as if the occupants have cleared out in a hurry. I look back at Momma. She nods and turns to leave. And I follow.

She shows me one other room downstairs. Its walls are lined with shelves that reach from floor to ceiling, all crammed with books. The wooden floor is scattered with pillows and cushions of all shapes, sizes and colours. The fire has been laid, but is unlit.

'This is the library. We come in here to read, or to play. The fire is lid in the evenings.'

I am bored. I want to see life. Pregnant women. Children. Not a houseful of empty rooms. If I want empty rooms, I can walk into any house in Dunham any time I like.

'Now we will go upstairs. Please follow.'

At last.

'I am afraid I cannod show you the birthing room or the nursery today. They must be kept as clean as possible. This is the meeding room.'

I am not clean enough for the House of the New Dawn.

She opens the door onto a room that is the physical embodiment of peace. Its walls are white but seem to glow with golden warmth, the reflection of an internal sun. Four long sofas form a square round a low table in the centre of the room. Unlit candles are dotted everywhere, hundreds of them. Just looking in makes me want to lie down.

'This is like a giant's house,' I say, 'for something to say.' All the furniture is huge. Big enough to accommodate a whole district. So where is everyone?

Momma indulges me with a smile but says nothing. I wait on the landing while she closes the door on the meeting room. Then she turns and starts back down the stairs. I stay where I am, in silent protest; there are four more doors on this landing, plus however many rooms there may be on the floor above. I still haven't met any of the inhabitants, apart from the stupid woman who let me in the other day. I stare at Momma, who waits for me on the stairs, then look over my shoulder in the direction I would rather go.

'I am sorry, but all the other rooms are private. Some of them you will nod see even when you come to live here.'

When, not if.

I give in and follow her down to the kitchen. Momma pours more tea, this time for both of us, and we reclaim our places at the table.

'Well, Rachel, whad do you think?'

I am lost for words, but suppress my indignation in favour of an attitude more likely to bring me into Momma's confidence.

'I think it's beautiful.'

'Do you still think you would like to join us?'

'Yes, very much.'

'Is there anything else you would like to know?'

So far as my interests are concerned, I have been told and shown nothing; where to start?

'There is one thing,' I say. 'Where are the children?'

'We do nod keep children here.'

'But where do they go? The babies, I mean.' Do they eat them? Why go to all that trouble if they aren't going to keep them?

'Please do nod worry, they do nod come to any harm. Quite the contrary.' I have no choice but to believe her.

Momma's tone changes. She stares at me until she is certain of having my full attention.

'Rachel, if you are going to come and live with us, there is something I must tell you first, but id is information that must never leave these four walls. Id concerns Jason.'

Jason again. I cannot hide my surprise. I blink, too many times.

'As I told you, we are in regular contact with him, and if you come here you will hear his name mentioned often.'

'Where is he?'

'I cannod tell you thad, but he is very well. He was a regular visidor here undil he left and his going away was connected to his work here.'

'His work? What work?'

Momma doesn't answer. Then, 'You know what we do here, Rachel.'

'Yes, you make candles. And babies.'

Everything is suddenly clear. The clouds in my head have parted and an over-zealous sun is burning my retinas. Jason wouldn't have a baby with me because he was busy fathering children here; because he *believed*, and probably still does *believe*, as Momma *believes*, that babies should only be born into a controlled environment, and that anyone living outside these four walls is an unfit mother.

'Jason build our school and now runs id.'

And fathered every child in it, no doubt. And *she* thinks I should find it all highly acceptable. I force a smile. I need to get away. It seems there is nowhere I can go that I am not forced to run away from.

'Good,' I say.

Momma smiles.

'When would you like to come? Just come and see me when you are ready, and we will prepare for you.'

'Soon,' is all I can muster. 'Never,' is what I mean.

My options have reduced to two and both of those revolve around White. Either I befriend him to cancel out his malevolence, kill him with kindness as Jason would say, or kill him the other, more effective way.

I notice nothing on the way home, not even the rain. Then I enter the house and my senses perk up. At the foot of the stairs I stop and look up; there are no visible traces of an intrusion, but it's as if the very molecules of the atmosphere have been disturbed, rearranged. Even with the map, I doubt White could have found me so quickly.

With a cold heart I remove my boots and sneak up the stairs, using the banister to lever myself over familiar creaks. Someone has been in, picking things up, holding them up to the light, and putting them down again in favour of something more interesting. They have disturbed the covers on the sofa, lifted them to their face, and smelled my scent on them. Their hand has hovered above the stove, detecting heat, calculating how long since it went out. They wished they could raise the shutters, shed some light on the movements of my daily life.

The key to the study is still in the drawer, but has not been replaced with the precision of an intruder. Jason. He is not far away, Momma said. He could be hiding, or out looking for me. Not so long ago I would have been relieved at the thought of his return, glad for him to step in and rescue the situation, knit together all the fraying threads of my life. But things have changed. I've changed. I waited, and he didn't come. And I'm not ready to confront him yet. If I saw him now I would kill him. And not with kindness.

I go down the stairs, my socks soaking up all the little puddles I dripped onto them on the way up. I grab my umbrella and shove my feet into my boots, not stopping to tie the strings, and leave the house as I found it. He is gone now, but he may come back.

Nowhere is safe now, but there is one place I can be certain of not being found by Jason: the place where my bag lies abandoned; White's house. I appreciate the irony of the situation. It is as if my final letting go of Jason has propelled him homewards after all. And how topsy-turvy that White's house should be my haven.

I take neither the lane nor my usual path through the park, but follow the park wall, the point of my umbrella prodding at the spongy earth, rain driving into the backs of my legs, wind pounding at the fabric over my ears. My route, wooded and thick with bracken, follows the course of the river over Home Farm land. My boot strings tangle with the long grass and catch up dead fiddleheads. My skirts cling heavy to my legs; the rain soaks through their flimsy protection and penetrates my bones.

I veer wide of Home Farm, but once through the trees am exposed in the open fields. At least the black and white dog can no longer give me away. I move through the rows of soya as quickly as my boots, heavy with mud, will allow. The farmhouse roof shines red against the livid sky as if lit by the evening sun; in this special light everything is visible. Everything except me, I hope.

I reach the road unaccosted. The warmth of the New Dawn house is just a short walk away. They would feed me. They would protect me from White. But not from Jason. And certainly not from themselves and their strange ideas. If I ever came close to surrendering, that moment has now long since passed.

Once I have crossed the river I am able to resume my trek across country with less risk of being seen. The way is long and arduous; I am hungry, thirsty, exhausted. Sobs scrape the back of my throat, tears merge with the raindrops that make such casual claims upon my body. Even the thought of my blanket or the remaining omelette, of the comfort they will provide when I reach my destination, cannot console me in the present. Tears slide the length of my nose and I realise I am crying; for all the feelings I have never owned: for fear, for anger, for loneliness. I think of all the people sleeping in the world; all those people in their safe little communities, with their precious children. I hate them; resent them for their warmth, their companionship, my exclusion.

The rain stops, while I trudge on. I gather up my skirts, wringing them out as I go, an act of punctuation at the end of the weather's long-drawn-out sentence, and inhale the after-rain smell.

A pair of rabbits appear out of the grey and scamper through the grass, tails flashing white; like the wind in the trees it is the effect of their movements on their surroundings, and not their physical presence, that is discernible in the twilight.

I take off my jacket and shake it out, welcoming the breeze that cools my sweating back; but my body is wholly dependent on clothes for its defence against the weather, and my temperature immediately drops. I swing my jacket round like a matador's cloak and hang it off my shoulders. The ground underfoot is marshy; great clumps of spiky grass stab at the air. I could easily lose my way in the dark, so at the first thinning in the hedge I squeeze through onto the road.

I have become aware of a strange humming sound, which I identify as my own voice; its tune is a random invention that provides the perfect accompaniment to my footsteps. Jason once said that singing is a natural function of humankind, designed to keep misery at bay. My display of a normal human response cheers me, and I keep time by tapping the umbrella point on the ground. I raise the volume to breaking point. Some people's singing voices bear no relation to their speaking voice. What does that say about those people and their relationship with their own misery? Unfortunately I cannot hold a thought for longer than a three-step round and the answer is lost.

By now Lymm, invisible against the backdrop of night, is behind me, and at last the land around me stretches out to meet the woodland that edges Noah's community. Almost there. I turn into Weaste Lane. My throat is parched from singing.

My bag is where I left it, its contents untouched. The omelette tastes better with age; I wash it down with water. In my upstairs room, I take off my wet trousers and skirts, wrap myself up tightly in the blanket and curl up on the floor to sleep. I have no plan. I dare not think of later, I think only of now.

21.9.43

Filthy and dark, her house stinks of decay. I thought I must be too late, that she would be lying there, dead and rotting. But she's disappeared. She lives like an animal. A filthy bitch. She'll have to live in the studio with the others. But I've lost her. If she hadn't gone to Momma I wouldn't have lost my grip. That woman persists in interfering with my romantic life even now.

7.05pm. full orgasm. standing.

Jason sits cross-legged, naked but for the long purple robe that has been passed over his head. Its silken fabric rests cool against the skin of his thigh, which by contrast is heating in anticipation of the forthcoming ritual. The presence of others is a tangible, scented chaos that he cannot forcibly draw into his nostrils, but rather must absorb as a hand plunged into a rushing stream assimilates the water's temperature.

He daren't allow his eyelashes to even flicker apart for a glimpse of them.

The sweet exhalations of their chanting brush his face, lift the soft hairs on his belly and turn the skin on his arms to gooseflesh. And then stop. All is still but for the twitching between his legs, his breathing heavy and self-conscious in the silence.

A voice. *O Sacred Seed, rise up and replenish this impoverished breed.*

Something light and cool, a hand, rests on the crown of his head. The light under his eyelids swims from red into purple into blue.

Bless our beloved Donor and Receptor, and bless this Dawn with a fruitful conception.

With the hand as its conductor, the voice resonates through the bones of his skull. The hand's fingers give the crown of his head a sharp tap, and the light behind

his eyes first greys, then silvers, and then floods his whole
being with a piercing white light that splinters into sprays
of stars. He watches for an eternity until a voice breaks the
silence and the stars fade away. A different voice.

You may open your eyes now.

The room, although lit by a thousand candles, is dull in
comparison to the display he has just witnessed in his head.
His torso is weightless, anchored to the floor by the stiff
triangle of his folded legs.

They have all gone. All except the body stretched
before him on the floor. The anonymous Receptor is
covered from head to toe in a cloth dyed purple to match
his own robe. A tiny protuberance, under which the cloth
flutters up and down in the breath of his accomplice,
marks the tip of her nose. Further along, two erect nipples
push at the cloth despite the heat of the fire.

He finds himself pushing his weight forward onto his
hands and rising up onto his knees so that his numb legs
unfold behind him. His thighs press in towards the soles of
the Receptor's feet, and they in turn yield as she raises her
knees skywards, allowing him to move further over her.

The tip of his erection seeks out the gash in the cloth
cover, but his hands are placed so as not to disturb either
it or the Receptor's body. His buttocks clench. His arms
shake under his own weight. He closes his eyes, but the
stars and lights have gone, he is in the world of purest
physicality, and the spell that has been cast over him and
his counterpart may be neither diverted nor broken.

It is done.

The voice speaks again from under the cloth, unfamiliar
and sterile. He had not even moved! He wants to ask if
she is sure, but that is not allowed. And she is of course

more finely tuned than him. It is a question of faith. He shudders, and pulls himself back onto his crossed legs, closing his eyes as he was instructed to do. His penis rests warm, limp and wet against his foot. Now the spell has been broken the floor is hard under his shins. All around him the air whispers with movement until at last a voice breaks the silence. Momma's voice.

You may open your eyes now.

Two arms support his and help him to his feet. The strength has been sapped from his legs. Momma stands smiling before him.

Bless you, she says.

She turns and leaves the room while he hobbles, aided by two senior acolytes, towards a steaming bath in the preparation room. His silent helpers assist in the removal of his robe and help him into the water, silky with oil. They leave him alone to conduct his sensory revival in private, and at last he allows himself a smile.

I come to with a start, woken by a movement in the room below. Instinct prevents me from making any sound. Curled up in the foetal position, I squint like a newborn in the daylight. My clothes are in a pile just out of reach. The drinking bottle lies on its side, tantalisingly close, but my arms are trapped between my legs, and I dare not move them. My umbrella is propped against the wall; a wet circle spread out from its tip like a shadow of its thin self.

He is in the kitchen, no doubt at the preparation of more grisly experiments. Dust tickles the roof of my mouth and I'm afraid I may cough, but if I reach for the water bottle he'll hear. And I need to pee. The two problems feed into one another; it is impossible to forget one by focusing on the other. I squeeze my thighs tighter together; my stomach hurts from the effort of controlling my bladder. I prepare myself for the possibility that I may have to piss into the already damp blanket.

Whatever he was doing he has now stopped and the cottage is quiet; the threat in silence is greater than the threat in action. I picture him, his chin raised to the ceiling, sensing my presence. For all I know he may already be aware I am here, may have discovered me while I slept, stood over me, watched my eyelids flicker as I dreamed of Jason, planned where to make his first incision.

His footsteps reverberate across the room below and stop in the hallway. I imagine him inspecting my footprints on the stairs. My eyes calculate the distance between me and my only weapon, the umbrella. But then the front door opens and his boots are scuffing up the path outside. I do not immediately shake off my blanket and crawl to the window for another look at him, the monster, but wait instead for the distant slam of his front door and confirmation of my safety.

Only then do I allow myself to stretch out a hand towards the bottle and take a few sips of my dwindling water supply to ease my scratched throat. The urge to urinate grows stronger. I wriggle free of my blanket and check the view from the window. His bike is propped against the side of the house. If he has already been out and come back I could be trapped in this room until nightfall. I am trapped until then anyway; I cannot risk another journey in daylight.

Unable to wait a moment longer, I crawl to a halfway point in the room, choose a spot against the outer wall, and squat down. Tiny specks of urine spatter my ankles, glisten like morning dew on the hairs of my legs. A warm green smell attaches itself to my next inbreath. I pass up the opportunity to inspect my work and instead get dressed and ready to assume my best watching position, squeezed into the corner by the window. The sky hangs heavy and unmoving, also waiting for the right moment. But White is prepared for a turn in the weather; he appears at his bicycle, dressed from head to foot in yellow waterproof clothing. His bag hangs off his shoulders like a deflated lung, stained dark at its base. By blood. His hair is hidden under a helmet. He is in disguise. I wonder how he keeps his hair short. He is a man out of time, an anachronism. While I have always been pinned down by the future, it is clear that he is locked into the past. He has fixed his creaking pedal; I don't hear him go. He too is a master of stealth.

I stretch up to my full height and raise my arms to the ceiling; my fingernail snags a flake of plaster and sends it fluttering down to settle in the dust like a snowflake in the desert. I give my jacket a vigorous shake, relishing the noise and the activity, then run my arms into its sleeves and pull it on, trapping a mat of hair against my back. I leave my boot strings untied.

His house is exactly as it was before, even down to the smell of fried eggs. All that has changed is my opinion of him, which hasn't so much changed as travelled a full circuit from disgust to loathing, stopping only briefly at mild sympathetic interest on the way.

The focus for my curiosity is now on his yellow book; my perspective on its contents has shifted. It is one thing to commit a foul act; it is quite another to record it for posterity. He repulses me. I sit myself down on the edge of his bed and open the journal at random. And straight away I find it. The answer to my questions contained in a handful of sinister words: *It has to be Divine Intervention. All those years of searching and hoping and I find it in her friend the ginger cat's den. Eight numbers on a tiny scrap of paper.*

It was White who called me. I already know it was White who called me, but I didn't know *how* he came to be calling me. Until I come to a new entry in the journal. I open and reopen the book at random. *She lives like an animal.*

So it was White not Jason who was in my house, snooping, picking at my belongings with his measly fingers. All the time I have been searching for him, he has been looking for me, watching me. Yes, I am an animal, and so are you. But you have forgotten and that is the difference between us. There is a symmetry to our lives that must be broken. Which of us is the quarry? Who is this Paloma that he refers to over and over, that he is preparing to capture and tame? It is me. I am Paloma. But I am not his. He has lost his advantage and he knows it.

At the top of the stairs I stop and listen to the house. Its silence has assumed a new menace, with the ticking clock as its heartbeat. I walk down the stairs and open the front door. I stab my feet into my boots, then run across to the cottage and slam the door behind me. I am Paloma. And this man, who is he? A man obsessed with time, with the desire to manipulate, to control his destiny and, more important, to capture mine.

For now he has me cornered, but not trapped. I plan to bide my time, to enjoy the present and leave when it is safe to do so. In other times the present was seen as an uncomfortable dead spot, an inconvenient moment to be endured in order to access the safety of hindsight. It was this fear of the present and the desire to fast-forward into a utopian future that forced the world to shift into reverse and move backwards faster than it ever had advanced. I will enjoy my wait. The scent of my urine lingers, intimate and comforting. The damp patch on the carpet disappears with the fading light.

The next thing I know, I am shaken awake by a bang that rattles the windows. Frantic raindrops pummel the glass, but it is not thunder that has brought me to my senses. It's him. He has just entered, or left, the cottage. My head is tight as with the advent of a storm. With a twitch of a movement I look out onto the lane. But there is no sign of him.

He is in his macabre workshop, cutting, stitching, his bloodied hands methodical in the gloom, putting the final touches to his latest masterpiece. He is dangerous now, I know that much. I am careful not to linger on any thought that might cast itself down and alert him to my presence. Instead I transmit psychic encouragement for him to return home; I visualise him in his house, in his kitchen, lowering the shutters, preparing for the night's retreat, writing in his diary, and then asleep. I picture myself leaving, closing the door behind me, and walking unaccosted towards the safety of Weaste Lane. Then I imagine him catching a glimpse of my escape and coming after me and I have to rewind and erase the scene. Then at last, at long last, my opportunity arrives.

Vertical rain attacks me without mercy for the duration of the trek home. Its pounding rhythm numbs my thoughts. I pass my umbrella from one aching arm to the other.

Dizzy with hunger, I would eat raw nettles if I could see to pick them. The remaining dribble at the bottom of my water bottle has developed a sulphur smell, but I ration it out, allowing myself tiny sips at predetermined points on the journey.

The house is open, doors gaping, lights on, as I left it. The hall stinks of festering nettle soup. I scream Jason's name up the stairs, just in case, and listen as it roams the house to return unanswered. On a stair halfway up is a scrap of brown paper. I throw off my jacket and boots, and crawl up to it, too weary for any display of enthusiasm. Up on the top step where the light is strongest, I unfold the note:

RACHEL, I THINK I HAVE SEEN HIM. SOMEONE WHO LOOKS LIKE THE MAN IN YOUR PAINTING CAME INTO THE MARKET TODAY ASKING IF I HAVE SEEN YOU. HE SEEMED WORRIED ABOUT YOU. I HOPE YOU ARE ALL RIGHT. PHONES OUT FOR GOOD NOW DID YOU KNOW? COME BY THE MARKET TOMORROW IF YOU ARE OK OR I WILL COME TO YOU. NOAH

This is not Noah's writing. I have seen Noah's writing; he is barely literate. I screw the paper into a ball, take it into the kitchen and throw it into the unlit stove. He is closing in and now I have to protect myself. Hunger tap-dances in my gut. I set about lighting the stove; one little corner of the house becomes warm and my spirits improve.

A rusty wet stain has appeared on the bathroom ceiling; the bucket in the loft has overflowed in the heavy rain. I ignore it for now and twist open the bath tap. Tea-coloured water gushes into the tub, exploring its confines like an animal released from captivity, only to find itself trapped in a larger pen. My fingers play in the tepid waterfall waiting for its temperature to change. When at last the warm water flows through, I ram the plug into the hole and the water level rocks higher. Tiny droplets of condensation form and then burst and run down the tiled walls. It was White who left that note, and he is planning to lie in wait for me somewhere between here and the market.

Now is the time to plunder Jason's neat store of folded sweaters and trousers, untouched since his departure and stacked in the airing cupboard. But first I warm my palms and then the backs of my hands on the water tank, turning them one way and then the other, then pressing them to my cheeks, my nose. Jason's clothes are mine now, with the exception of a few things I never liked. I pull out a plain white T-shirt, a grey woollen sweater and heavy black cotton trousers with pockets at each thigh. Careful to avoid contact with my own soiled and threadbare clothes, I spread the T-shirt over the water tank to warm and lay the rest out on the bed. The clothes I have worn constantly since Jason left are ragged and stinking with ingrained dirt; they can all be burned. I will take all the clothes from the wardrobe to the market another day.

The bath water is running cold again so I shut off the tap. It is a long time since I saw my naked body; I peer over the loose flesh at my midriff to my protruding feet, one of which, I notice, is thrown out at an odd angle.

The heat stings my shins as I lower myself to a squat in the bath; a rush of my own fluid escapes from between my legs. Slowly I unfold into the warmth and immerse myself; breasts, shoulders, face, all disappear under the surface.

My hair sighs out into the water, my stick legs waver, rejuvenated breasts bob. Two black-headed toes peek up into the bell of the tap, and my knees break the surface of the water like newly risen barren islands. All my aches and chills seep out into the water.

If White thinks he can trick me by luring me into a trap, he has a surprise coming. He can wait all day; I won't be going to the market. I grab the lump of soap from the end of the bath and rub its hardened crust into my palm until it begins to froth. I stroke the lather a palmful at a time over my head, working it in with my fingers. I duck under the water and attempt to untangle the knots in my hair.

Then with a great splash I sit up, hook a big toe round the chain of the stopper and yank it from the plughole. The water swirls below the level of the greasy tidemark that rings the bath; I ease myself to my feet and dry myself on the pink towel. My cheeks are rosy with the heat, and tiny beads of sweat cling to the hairs of my upper lip. I tie a ponytail using one of Jason's socks. With my clean hair I am strangely weightless, taller, light-headed. I am resolved. I am clear. I will be absolved. I don't need Momma to shield me from White. I don't need White to shield me from Jason. I don't need any of them.

The sky has yet to give way to the inevitable approach of morning. A simmering concoction steams up the kitchen window; drool wets the corners of my mouth. The last of the bread is petrified to the density of rock; I stab optimistically at its surface several times then flash it under the tap and place it in the oven. I write a backwards hello in the condensation on the window and wonder how many days I have spent walking from window to window, staring out without seeing, over the field to the park, over the river to the canal, seeing nothing at all. Now I know he was out there all the time, watching me, from the canal path, from the lane, even from the walkway, taking note of every detail of my life. Hoping to be seen.

I ladle soup into a bowl then wipe the message from the window. It is important that he should continue to believe me gone. I must make a clear plan and act quickly.

Rain hammers against the shutters. I busy myself with my chores, occasionally feeding a ripped skirt or a holed jumper into the stove to keep me warm one last time.

After a few more spoonfuls of soup, eaten straight from the pan, I settle down on the sofa for a nap, under grubby and dust-ridden covers. When all this is over I will wash them, and hope they don't fall apart.

For the first time since all this began, I know what to do next. I am ready to do what I must and set off on my bike with my umbrella poking out from either side of my rucksack. I take the long route. On any other day variation would have made the journey more interesting but today I have no mind for taking in the scenery. I hide my bike by the hawthorn as before, and pass through into his territory for the last time. I know he is not here, he is watching for me on the road to the market.

In the cottage, the scent of urine still hangs in the air, marking my own little territory within his. I take the umbrella, torch and water bottle from my bag. Everything else I leave behind. I hook the umbrella over my arm and walk over to the house. I remove my boots at the door but this time I carry them with me up the stairs, matching my footsteps to the march of the ticking clock as I climb.

I check he isn't sleeping in the blue room, then go into the pink room, and drop my belongings on the floor. I take a swig of water then stash the bottle, boots and torch under the bed.

Next, I look for a place to hide myself.

Behind the door is a cupboard, empty but for a shelf at eye level with a hanging rail fixed to its underside. The space beneath it is tall enough to crouch in and not very deep, but it will do.

The blue room is unchanged. He is a meticulous man. I perch on the edge of the bed and pick up the yellow book. There are no new entries and I cannot bear to read the old ones again. I replace the book on the table. There is nothing to do now but wait.

I cross the landing to the pink room and my attention switches for a moment to the scene outside the window, to the ominous peace outside, where the earth holds its breath. In his room, the clock ticks louder, counting down to his inevitable, and possibly imminent, return. The light on his bedside table comes on automatically. Soon he will come.

I move the torch and umbrella from under the bed and put them in the cupboard, torch on shelf, umbrella propped in the back corner, spike downwards. Then I drag the wooden chair over to the window and sit down to watch for his return. The lane disappears under darkness but still he doesn't come. It makes me smile to imagine him out there, hiding behind a tree, waiting to pounce on me. Our symmetry is still intact. We were both seeking and now we are both hiding.

My legs and back ache, which is only to be expected, and my sitting bones rub uncomfortably against the wooden seat, but I dare not move or sleep for fear of missing his arrival.

At last I hear a movement out in the lane, the crunch of his bicycle on the stony path. I spring into action, feeling my way across the room towards the cupboard. But he doesn't come in straight away, and I hope he hasn't found some evidence of me out there in the lane to forewarn him. I venture back to the window. There is a light moving in the downstairs window of the cottage, in the kitchen. The light fades, and I expect to hear the door bang shut, but instead the light appears in the upstairs window, the window of my room, where my things are. Now he is coming.

The front door opens, but he doesn't call out. I freeze, gauging his movements. His actions are slow and heavy; he fills something with water. A muted hum drifts up the stairs, less tuneful than a droning bee. He is singing.

Under the cover of his caterwauling I sneak into the cupboard. The umbrella knocks against the wall. I pull at the door but cannot close it completely; there is no handle on the inside, but I am able to hold it in place by gripping at the moulding with the tips of my fingers.

The smell of frying onions follows his tuneless misery up the stairs and I wonder where he finds food if he doesn't use the market. He must have his own plot of land somewhere, or maybe just helps himself to other people's, not that anyone would care. The latter seems most likely. My mouth is watering.

A stronger, dirtier smell overpowers the fruitiness of the onions. Meat. Too strong to be rabbit. I guess it's fox. Or dog. Both are safe. Rabbit retribution was Jason's name for the cause of the deaths of thousands of city people during the crisis. People who died from starvation because their diet consisted of nothing but rabbit. People so detached from nature they knew no better.

Things are quieter below; he must be eating, his little mouth working away at the stringy meat, his eyes greedy for nourishment, his breath taking on the character of the seared flesh. Next comes the clatter of dishes as he clears away at the end of his meal. My discomfort is absolute; I will him to go to bed. *Go to bed. Go to bed.*

He closes the downstairs shutters and throws the bolt on the front door. He leaves the house open while he is out, but locks himself in at night. Then I count his dejected footsteps on the stairs. Four. Five. I have left the chair by the window. Eight. There is nothing I can do now; it is in the hands of fate.

Fear is not such an unpleasant sensation; I fail to understand why people are so frightened of it. He is at the top of the stairs now. He stops and I think for one dreadful moment that he knows where I am and is pretending not to. He mumbles something I cannot hear and turns into the blue room. He winds something, his torch, or the clock. Then the wall behind me knocks as he climbs into bed. I know from his journal that he sleeps in his clothes; just as I know he will usually get up at least once in the night to change them, or to masturbate, or both. There is the rustle of paper as he makes his final entry in his yellow book. My legs are cramping. The book rattles as he closes it again. No more than the width of a brick separates his head and my back; I dare not even blink in case the movement reverberates through to his consciousness.

A purring, the sound of sleep, like trickling water, accompanies the ticking clock. There is no other sound, not even an isolated rap at the wall as he shifts position. I relax my grip on the door and let it swing open and stretch out my aching fingers.

My room is lit only by the spillage from his bedside lamp. He sleeps with the light on: a man afraid of the dark. I wait a few moments then climb out of the cupboard, holding the umbrella before me like a spear, and tiptoe to a new position behind the door. A pathway of light runs from his doorway, and dissolves in the shadows of the pink room, beckoning me into his.

But not yet. I creep to the cupboard and switch on the torch, turning the beam to the wall so that a secondary reflected glow gives out just enough light for me to work by. I carry the wooden chair in slow motion across the room. Pausing to allow my eyes time to adjust to the stronger light, I cross the landing.

He is shielded from view by the door. I stifle my own breathing to hear his more clearly and the duet of snoring and ticking urges me on. I take one quick step into his room.

He is asleep on his side, facing me. He sleeps close to the light; a man afraid of death. And but for the snoring, he is so still he could be already dead. The innocence of his sleeping face belies his true nature. I watch for a flickering eyelid, for any sign of pretence. Imagine his confusion if he were to wake now, to the sight of a chair floating in mid-air, followed by his Paloma, his Nemesis, sleepwalking with funereal grace to be at his side when he awakes. He would see me place the chair at his bedside, level with his heart.

I return to the pink room, roll the drinking bottle from under the bed and place it by the door with my boots. I rise slowly and turn back to his room.

I raise one foot onto the seat of the chair, find my balance then pull the other foot up behind it, wobbling dangerously. I find my balance and shuffle myself around until I stand directly above him. My own breathing has stopped.

I grip the umbrella with both hands, more to keep my hands from shaking than to hold the umbrella steady. The metal point hovers for an instant above his upturned earhole like a hungry sparrowhawk.

I purse my lips and plunge, pushing my whole weight down onto the umbrella, its stalk buckling beneath me. The point disappears into his skull. His eyes and mouth fly open as I work the umbrella from side to side.

A bright red bubble appears in the corner of his ear; a bloody stream misses the gully that runs from nose to mouth and spills over his cheek. I look away but keep on with my stirring; grinding with all my might, entranced, until at last my aching muscles scream at me to stop.

I am standing on the bed, straddling the bulk of his torso, hands still clinging to the umbrella. I tug at it but it refuses to budge. My hands drop away, the skin of my palms blistering already. My entire body trembles as I step back onto the chair then down onto solid ground. He has one eye open and the other shut. Out of respect I avert my curious gaze from the bed, grab the yellow book and stumble out of the room.

I gather up my things then flee down the stairs, out of the front door and into the cottage. I stop only to pull on my jacket and ram the book into my rucksack, then run for the tunnel. It's a shame about the umbrella, all bent and useless. He can keep it as a souvenir of our relationship. Although I doubt he'll have much use for it where he's going.

23.9.43

I have waited, and you have come.

WE GOT TO THE HOUSE FIRST THING IN THE MORNING BEFORE THE MARKET. SHADY KNEW WHAT THE SMELL WAS STRAIGHT AWAY AND FOUND US BOTH A TOWEL FROM THE KITCHEN TO WRAP ROUND OUR HEADS AND COVER OUR NOSE AND MOUTH. IT IS THE TIDIEST HOUSE I'VE EVER SEEN. LIKE NO ONE LIVES IN IT. THE BODY WAS UPSTAIRS IN ONE OF THE BEDROOMS. WE CHECKED EVERY ROOM IN THE HOUSE BUT THERE WAS NOBODY ELSE THERE. IT WAS OBVIOUS WHO HAD DONE IT. TO ME ANYWAY. I RECOGNISED THE UMBRELLA.

I FIRST GOT SUSPICIOUS WHEN SHADY SAID HE HAD SEEN TWO STRANGERS IN ONE DAY. THE WOMAN WAS FRIENDLY AND SAID SHE WAS LOOKING FOR A DOG BUT SMELLED QUITE BAD AND LOOKED ILL. SHE WAS VERY THIN AND TALL AND HER CLOTHES WERE RAGGED A REAL SCARECROW OF A WOMAN HE SAID. SHE TOLD SHADY ANOTHER NAME BUT FROM THE DESCRIPTION I GUESSED IT WAS RACHEL. THIS WAS AFTER WE HAD SORTED OUT THAT JEZ WHITE WAS THE SAME MAN THAT HAD ESCAPED FROM THE NEW DAWN HOUSE AND I THOUGHT SHE WAS HAPPY WITH THAT AND WAS GOING TO LEAVE IT. THE SECOND STRANGER WAS A MAN. HE RODE PAST OUR COMMUNITY ON HIS BIKE JUST AFTER

SHE LEFT. SHADY DIDN'T SEE HIS FACE BECAUSE HE WAS GOING TOO FAST AND HAD HIS HEAD DOWN BUT IF IT WAS SOMEONE WE KNEW HE WOULD HAVE STOPPED NOT SPEEDED UP SO HE KNEW IT WAS A STRANGER. AND HE ONLY HAD ONE SMALL BAG ON HIM SO HE WASN'T A JOBBER. I KNOW EVERYONE IN THIS DISTRICT BUT I DIDN'T KNOW WHO HE WAS SO IT MUST BE THE SAME MAN RACHEL WAS LOOKING FOR. I WAS TRYING TO HELP HER AT FIRST BECAUSE I THOUGHT SHE MUST REALLY LIKE HIM AND SHE ALWAYS SEEMS SO LONELY AND MISERABLE. THEN I GOT WORRIED BECAUSE I THOUGHT HE MIGHT BE SPYING ON RACHEL AND WAS RIDING FAST TO GET AWAY BEFORE SHE SAW HIM. I WAS GOING TO TALK TO RACHEL ABOUT IT WHEN SHE NEXT CAME TO THE MARKET. ONLY SHE DIDN'T COME AND AFTER A FEW DAYS I STARTED TO GET WORRIED. IT WAS ON MY MIND TO GO TO HER HOUSE. SHADY SAID HE WOULD COME WITH ME. THEN WHITE TURNED UP IN THE MARKET ASKING IF I KNEW HER. I PRETENDED NOT TO KNOW WHO HE WAS AND HE PRETENDED HE HAD COME A LONG WAY TO SEE HER BUT HE HAD NO BAGS WITH HIM EXCEPT A SMALL RUCKSACK. I TOLD HIM I HAD NOT SEEN RACHEL FOR MANY DAYS. I COULDN'T WORK OUT IF HE WAS UPSET OR ANGRY SO I SAID I WOULD PASS ON A MESSAGE IF I SAW HER. HE SAID NOT TO BOTHER HE WAS SURE HE WOULD FIND HER. HE LEFT ON A BIKE JUST AS SHADY ARRIVED AT THE MARKET SO I MADE HIM FOLLOW TO SEE WHERE HE WENT. THEN I DECIDED TO LEAVE A NOTE AT RACHEL'S HOUSE. I THOUGHT IT WOULD PROBABLY BRING HER OUT OF HIDING IF I COULD TELL HER WHERE

HE IS. IF SHE DIDN'T TURN UP AT THE MARKET AFTER THAT I WOULD GET REALLY WORRIED.

WHEN SHADY CAME BACK HE SAID HE HAD FOLLOWED HIM TO A HOUSE NEAR THE CANAL. MY WRITING ISN'T VERY GOOD SO SHADY ALWAYS WRITES ANYTHING IMPORTANT AND I GOT HIM TO WRITE THE NOTE TELLING HER I HAD SEEN HIM AND FOR HER TO COME THE NEXT DAY. THEN I LEFT HIM IN CHARGE OF THE MARKET WHILE I WENT TO RACHEL'S. WHEN I GOT THERE A LITTLE CART WAS ON ITS SIDE IN THE LANE. THERE DIDN'T SEEM TO BE ANYTHING WRONG WITH IT. I THOUGHT I WOULD ASK RACHEL IF I COULD USE IT FOR THE MARKET. THE DOOR TO THE HOUSE WAS OPEN SO I WENT IN INSTEAD OF LEAVING THE NOTE OUTSIDE. I SHOUTED OUT BUT THERE WAS NO ANSWER. IT WAS VERY COLD IN THE HOUSE AND IT SMELLED QUITE BAD LIKE ROTTING VEGETABLES. I DIDN'T GO UP I JUST LEFT THE NOTE ON THE STAIRS AND WENT BACK TO THE MARKET. I WAS GOING TO GIVE HER ONE MORE DAY AND THEN THOUGHT I WOULD START LOOKING FOR HER. THE NEXT DAY SHE DIDN'T SHOW UP SO WHEN I GOT HOME FROM THE MARKET I TALKED TO SHADY ABOUT IT. SHADY SAID NOAH LET'S VISIT HIM FIRST BECAUSE FOR ALL WE KNOW THEY MAY HAVE MET UP AND BE TOGETHER IN WHICH CASE PROBLEM SOLVED. I AGREED THAT WAS THE BEST THING TO DO. AND THAT'S HOW WE FOUND THE BODY.

WE WRAPPED HIM UP IN THE BEDCLOTHES AND CARRIED HIM DOWN THE STAIRS AND LEFT HIM ON THE KITCHEN TABLE. SHADY SAID WE SHOULD BUILD A BONFIRE AND BURN IT AS SOON AS POSSIBLE BECAUSE IT

WAS ALREADY ROTTING. EITHER THAT OR CHOP IT UP AND BURN IT IN THE STOVE. THERE IS A PATCH OF GRASS BESIDE THE HOUSE WHERE WE BUILT THE FIRE. THE GRASS WAS VERY WET BUT THERE WAS A GOOD STORE OF DRY LOGS SO WE WERE ABLE TO GET THE FIRE GOING WITHOUT TOO MUCH TROUBLE. ONCE IT HAD CAUGHT PROPERLY WE FETCHED THE BODY AND THREW IT ON. THE HAIR WENT UP FIRST THE SMELL WAS WRETCHED. SHADY SAID WE HAD TO STAY AND WATCH IN CASE IT PUT THE FIRE OUT BUT THE STENCH WAS MAKING ME FEEL SO SICK I LEFT HIM FOR A WHILE TO GET SOME FRESH AIR. I COULD STILL SMELL IT ALL THE WAY DOWN THE LANE LIKE COOKING MEAT. WHEN I GOT BACK SHADY HAD BEEN SICK TOO. WE BOTH AGREED IT WAS THE WORST THING WE HAVE EVER HAD TO DO. IT REMINDED US OF THE OLD DAYS WITH THE BIG FIRES. WHEN ALL THE FLESH HAD GONE FROM THE BONES WE BROUGHT BUCKETS OF WATER FROM THE HOUSE TO PUT OUT THE FIRE. SHADY SAID WE MIGHT NEED TO SHOW THE BONES AS PROOF. THEN WE WENT TO RACHEL'S HOUSE. I HARDLY RECOGNISED RACHEL WHEN I SAW HER, SHE WAS CLEAN AND HAD ON DIFFERENT CLOTHES AND SHE LOOKED HAPPY. SHADY SHOWED HER WE HAD HER UMBRELLA BUT REFUSED TO LET HER HAVE IT BACK. SHE INVITED US IN. I HAVE ALWAYS BEEN A BIT SCARED OF RACHEL. HER HOUSE WAS NOW ALSO VERY TIDY AND SHE HAD ALL THE WINDOWS OPEN. WE ASKED HER WHY SHE DID IT AND SHE SAID WAIT A MINUTE I'VE GOT SOMETHING TO SHOW YOU. SHE DISAPPEARED UPSTAIRS AND THEN CAME BACK BRINGING A YELLOW BOOK THAT SHE SAID SHE TOOK FROM HIS HOUSE. SHE

GAVE IT TO US TO READ. HE WAS GOING TO KILL ME SHE SAID. HE KILLED ALL THE ANIMALS. I CAN SHOW YOU. SHADY TOOK THE BOOK AND READ BITS OUT TO ME THAT SHE SHOWED HIM. IT DID SEEM FROM THE BOOK THAT HE MIGHT HAVE KILLED HER IF SHE HADN'T GOT TO HIM FIRST BUT SHADY SAID THAT WE SHOULD WRITE DOWN EVERYTHING WE KNOW AND THEN TAKE IT TO ALL THE COMMUNITIES WITH THE BOOK AND THE UMBRELLA AND LET THEM DECIDE WHAT SHOULD HAPPEN NEXT. WE DIDN'T KNOW WHAT TO DO ABOUT RACHEL SO WE TOOK HER TO THE MARKET AND LOCKED HER IN. I GOT LOCKED IN ONCE AND I KNOW IT IS IMPOSSIBLE TO GET OUT OF THERE WITHOUT HELP. SHADY WROTE DOWN WHAT HAD HAPPENED SO FAR AND WE SET OFF. THE NEW DAWNERS PLACE IS CLOSEST TO THE MARKET SO THAT'S WHERE WE WENT FIRST. MOMMA GAVE US TEA AND SOME BREAD AND CHEESE WHICH WAS VERY NICE OF HER. SHADY READ HER THE STORY. MOMMA SAID THAT RACHEL HAD BEEN TO VISIT A FEW TIMES BECAUSE SHE WANTS TO LIVE WITH THEM. SHE SAID THAT SHE THOUGHT LONELINESS HAD DRIVEN RACHEL TO MURDER AND THAT IT MIGHT BE GOOD FOR RACHEL TO LIVE THERE FROM NOW ON. THEY WOULD LOOK AFTER HER. SHE SAID THAT JEZ WHITE WAS A STRANGE MAN AND THAT SHE HAD BEEN VERY CONCERNED WHEN RACHEL TOLD HER THEY WERE FRIENDS. SHE HAD THROWN HIM OUT OF THE NEW DAWN HOUSE BECAUSE HE WAS SCARING ONE OF THE WOMEN. NOW IT WAS CLEAR TO HER THAT RACHEL HAD BEEN SCARED OF WHITE TOO SHE COULD UNDERSTAND WHY SHE WOULD DO SUCH

A THING. MOMMA SAID THERE WAS NO DOUBT IN HER MIND THAT JEZ WHITE WAS A DANGEROUS MAN. NEXT WE WENT TO HOME FARM AND SPOKE TO EVERYONE THERE. THEY ALL THOUGHT IT WAS A VERY GOOD IDEA THAT RACHEL SHOULD GO AND LIVE WITH THE NEW DAWNERS. EVERYONE THINKS THAT SHE HAS BEEN ILL FOR A VERY LONG TIME AND NEEDS TO BE LOOKED AFTER. SOME OF THE HOME FARMERS KNEW JASON AND THEY SAID HE LEFT BECAUSE HE COULDN'T STAND IT WITH HER ANY MORE. THEY SAID THEY HAD THOUGHT SHE MUST BE GETTING BETTER BECAUSE THEY HAD SEEN HER OUT AND ABOUT RECENTLY BUT NOW THEY COULD SEE IT WAS PROBABLY BECAUSE SHE WAS GETTING WORSE. THE OLDER MEMBERS OF THE COMMUNITY HAD SEEN JEZ WHITE'S HOUSE WHEN THEY WERE LOOKING FOR SOMEWHERE TO SETTLE IN THE AREA WHEN THEY HAD TO MOVE OUT OF THEIR VANS BUT THE HOUSE WAS TOO SMALL FOR THEM AND THEY HAD NEVER MET OR EVEN HEARD OF JEZ WHITE. AT FOXLEYHALL THE MAIN IDEA WAS THAT SHE SHOULD EITHER BE KILLED HERSELF OR PUT AWAY SOMEWHERE SAFE. NOBODY THERE HAD EVER MET RACHEL OR JASON BUT THEY SAID THAT A STRANGE WOMAN HAD BEEN HANGING AROUND AND FRIGHTENING THE CHILDREN. THEY HAD NEVER HEARD OF JEZ WHITE. WHEN WE TOLD THEM THAT MOMMA HAD OFFERED FOR RACHEL TO GO AND LIVE THERE THEY THOUGHT THAT IT WOULD BE GOOD BECAUSE THEN SHE WOULD LIVE WITH ALL THE OTHER NUTTERS AND PERHAPS SHE MIGHT KILL SOME OF THEM OFF. WE WENT BACK TO SEE MOMMA WHEN WE HAD FINISHED TO TELL

HER THAT WE WOULD BRING RACHEL THAT DAY. SHE SAID HER BED WOULD BE READY AND THAT SHE SHOULDN'T BRING ANY BELONGINGS WITH HER. RACHEL WANTED TO FETCH A BOOK FROM THE MILL BUT WE SAID NO THAT WASN'T ALLOWED BUT OTHER THAN THAT SHE SEEMED QUITE HAPPY TO GO. SHE HAD MADE US TEA AND FRIED POTATOES AT THE MARKET WHICH WE ALL ATE THEN TOOK HER TO THE NEW DAWNERS' PLACE. I HAVE NEVER SEEN HER AGAIN AND NOR HAS SHADY.

THIS IS THE TRUTH.

TOLD BY NOAH AND WRITTEN BY SHADY FROM WEASTE LANE COMMUNITY.

Acknowledgements

Kate Evans' comic *Funny Weather* (also published by Myriad Editions) is essential reading and the most clear and accessible explanation of climate change I have found (*www.cartoonkate.co.uk*).

I am indebted to Dawn Linden for pulling the diary from the dumpster in deepest Pennsylvania and thinking of me.

In the course of writing this novel, the following people have given their invaluable support and encouragement and I send them love and thanks:

Stephanie Kaye, Sarah Barron-Pell, KP Parker, Astrid Williamson, Claire Gilliver, Sophie Hannah, Lenny Kaye, Moira Brown, Clare Grady, Trudy McGuigan, Michael Schmidt, Liz Kessler, Julie Brown, all in my Manchester Metropolitan University MA creative writing group, Niamh Dowling, Kate Engineer, John Knight, Sophie Ansar, Steve Murphy, Beatrice Ellis, Sue Forrest, Nicky Fijalkowska, Robert, Nick, Amanda, Stuart Deeks, Pete Fijalkowski, Jayne Houghton, Nicky Harper, Jean-Daniel Beauvallet, Lorna Thorpe, Rachel Rooney, Toyin Manley.

Special thanks to Heather Gratton; my agent Philippa Brewster and all at Capel & Land; and Candida Lacey, Vicky Blunden, Corinne Pearlman and Linda McQueen plus everyone else at Myriad Editions, without whom this book would not have seen the light of day.

And last, but always first, to my son Ben.

AFTERWORD:

What made you begin the novel?

The initial motivation for writing this story came from a growing frustration at the treatment climate change (aka global warming) predictions were given in the media at the time. Reports tended towards the trivialisation of supposed positives, and speculated about how fantastic the ensuing temperature rises would be because we'd all be able to save money by growing our own grapes and staying at home for holidays instead of drinking French wine and jetting off to the Mediterranean. I decided to make certain that I wasn't the only person to be scared by the prospect of increases in extreme weather (of all kinds) and rising sea levels, and so I set out to try to scare a few more.

But *I have waited* isn't a novel about climate change, it's about the impact of extreme change on one (fictitious) person's environment and their behaviour. *I have waited* is a novel about weather-induced madness.

What encouraged you along the way?

High winds and wild weather.

How important was research to the writing of the novel?

I read a lot of what was at the time current research into climate change, and met a few people engaged in that research. When I realised that nobody could state unequivocally what was going to happen, I used what I'd learned as a touchstone, and made it all up.

Scientific predictions about a climate-changed future tended to concentrate, understandably, on single causes and outcomes, all of which were frightening in their own right, but when separated off from one another appeared manageable if tackled by progressive technologies. Fiction can do what science can't by openly speculating about what kind of cocktail those single causes and outcomes might create if shaken up together, with a healthy dose of imagination and wishful thinking stirred in.

Did you visit the locations you were writing about?

I used to live on the edges of Dunham Massey park so I knew the area well enough, but since I left it's continued to be a favourite place to visit. I made a point of going back while I was writing, especially during the foot and mouth outbreak in 2001, to witness the park in a wilder, more overgrown state not dissimilar to the way I imagined it in the novel.

The principal reason for setting *I have waited* there was that the location lent itself well to the theme of isolation and disconnection I wanted to establish in the story. I lived in an old Victorian flour mill, which was at that time in a state of semi-renovation and, with a minimal shift of perspective, was easily re-imagined as semi-derelict.

It is easy to understand how, in the novel, Jason envisaged the mill as a place of self-sufficiency and peace, positioned as it was (and still is) on a tiny island in a river at the edge of a National Trust park, and as a modern gated community in embryo it required only a simple twist of reality to reconstruct it as a fortress, designed to keep out weather and human marauders alike. My deep familiarity with the setting allowed for the combination of memory and imagination in its recreation and, for me at least, this mixture helped to create a dreamlike (or nightmarish) atmosphere, in which the unknown and the feared haunt the known and the tenable.

Setting the story in a place I know well gave it a solid foundation upon which I could build the imaginary events of the novel. Later in the writing process, I was able to tweak the details of the location to suit the needs of the story, and readers who know the area around Dunham Massey well will notice that I took a few liberties with the greater geography (I defy anyone to drive from Dunham to Edale in twenty minutes with the weather in high dudgeon and in a vehicle which is effectively a solar-powered sewing machine on tractor wheels) – but it is a work of fiction after all.

In what ways did you draw on your own experiences in the writing of the book?

The mill, when I lived there in the early nineties, was mostly unpopulated but for me and my toddler son and the weekend walkers who liked to peer in at our windows (hence, perhaps, the theme of watching and being watched in the novel), not realising the mill was in part occupied (I'm being generous; they can't have missed my car parked outside).

In the novel, Rachel is the mill's solitary inhabitant and my own experience of having lived there helped, years later, in the reinvention of it as a place of threat and paranoia, in keeping with Rachel's volatile mental state.

In the main it was my intention to imagine a world that looked not dissimilar to the one we inhabit at the turn of the 21st century, but one in which humanity was no longer the dominant force, and where human behaviour was dictated by nature in general and the weather in particular.

Did any object, visual image or piece of music inspire the writing of the novel, or provide a reference point along the way?

Jeff Wall's *A Sudden Gust of Wind (after Hokusai)* was on the wall above my writing table and I spent a long time staring at it, but throughout the writing process I had a strong – I would say almost cinematic – visual sense of the novel, as if I was writing the score to a sequence of moving images on a screen.

How did you decide on the structure of the novel?

I first learned about structuring a longer piece of work by studying screenwriting, so deciding on the structure for *I have waited* involved much shuffling of index cards and plot points. As the story progressed I made the decision to keep it short and intense to reflect Rachel's claustrophobic existence so I read a few thrillers and tried to copy their structure to keep it concise and maintain as much tension as possible.

What was most challenging about the writing of the book?

The whole process was challenging, but the hardest thing was stopping as it still didn't feel finished to me, even at the point of publication. It was great to have the opportunity to make a few revisions for this second edition. At last I no longer feel I have unfinished business with this novel.